A Medieval Book of Days

A Medieval Book of Days

From the editors of
Renaissance Magazine

Phantom Press Publications
Nantucket, Massachusetts

Printed in Canada.

ISBN 0-9644759-1-X

RENAISSANCE MAGAZINE
80 Hathaway Drive
Stratford, CT 06615-7304

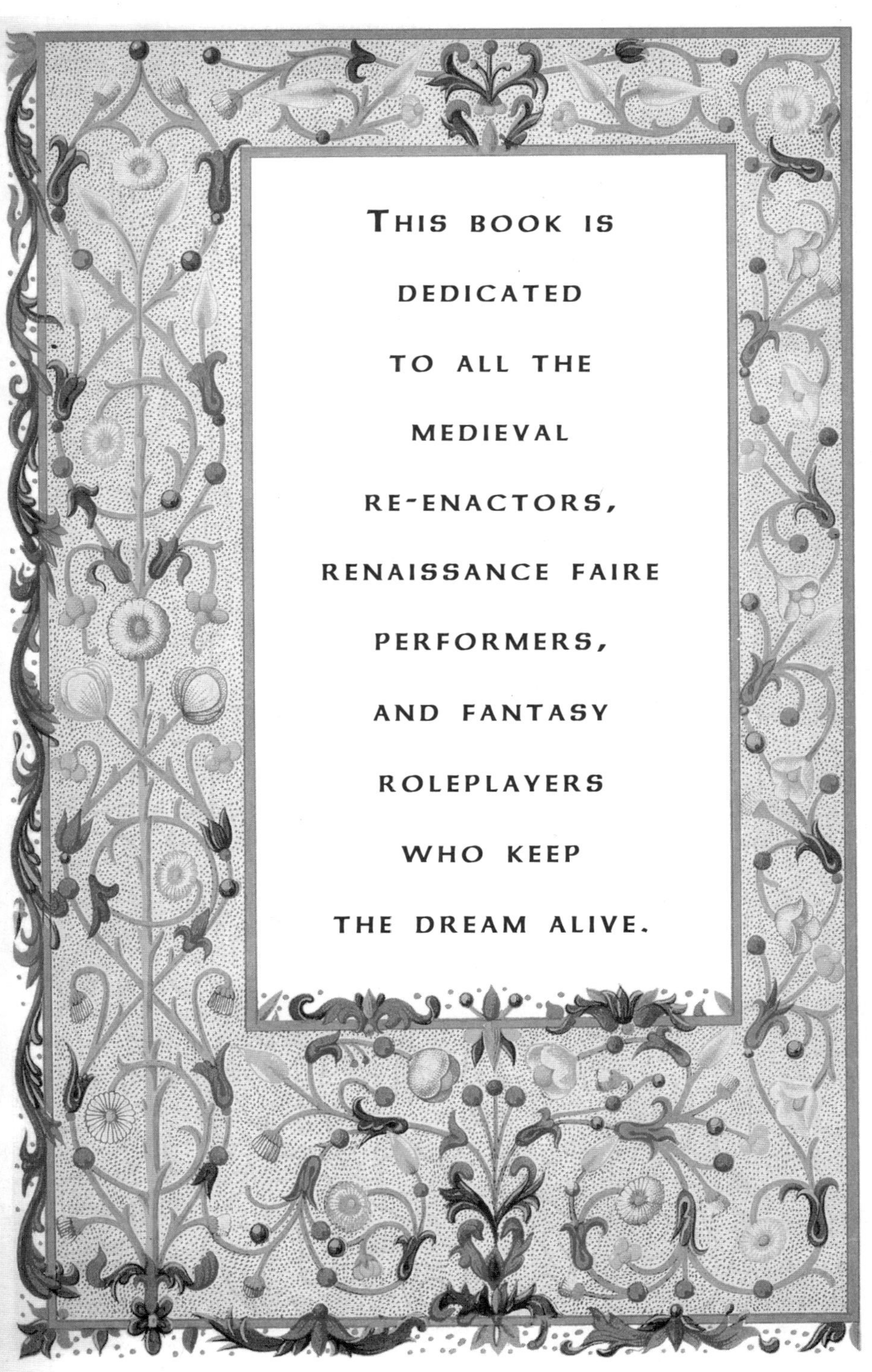

THIS BOOK IS DEDICATED TO ALL THE MEDIEVAL RE-ENACTORS, RENAISSANCE FAIRE PERFORMERS, AND FANTASY ROLEPLAYERS WHO KEEP THE DREAM ALIVE.

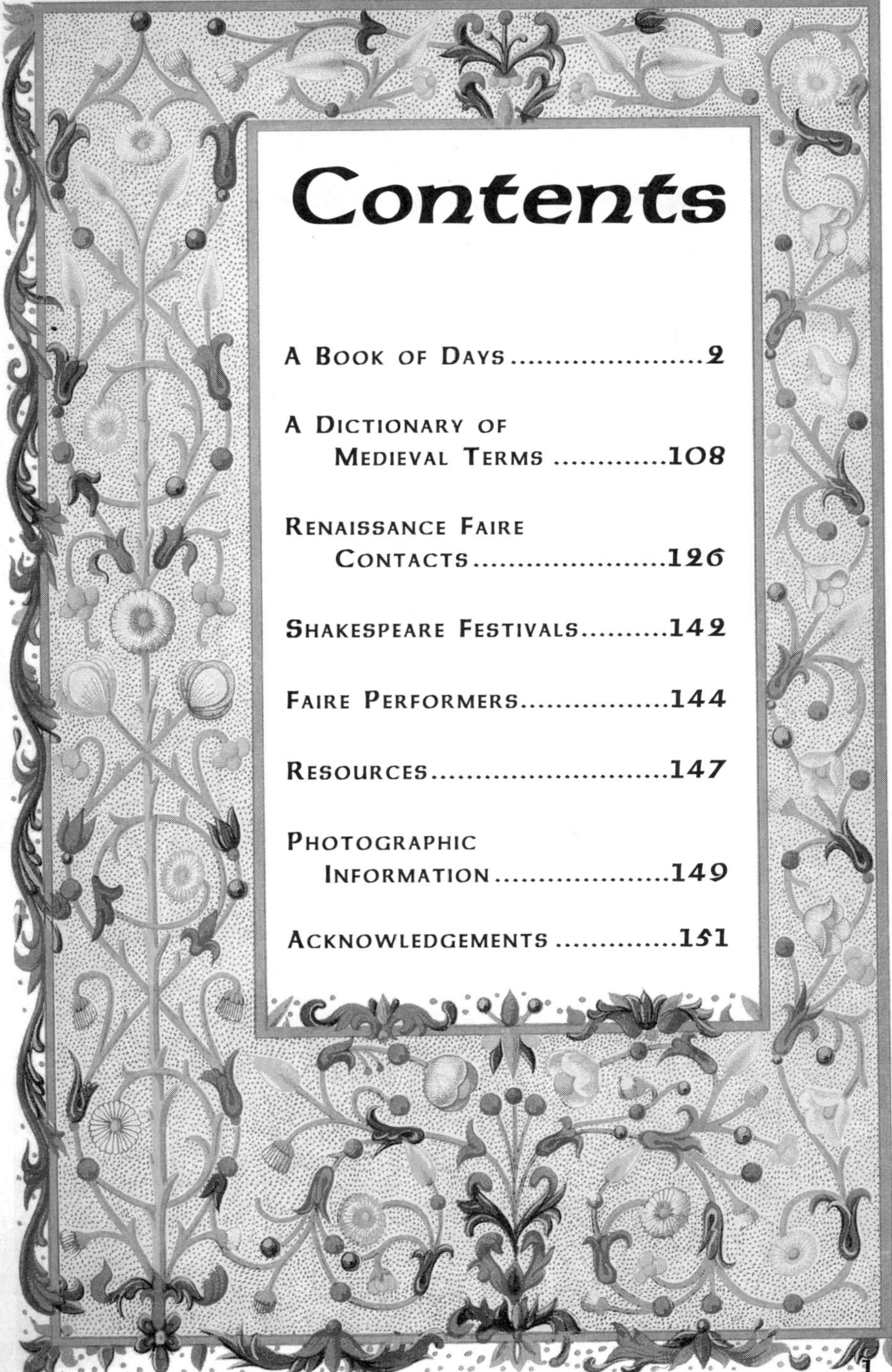

Contents

A Book of Days 2

A Dictionary of Medieval Terms 108

Renaissance Faire Contacts......................126

Shakespeare Festivals..........142

Faire Performers..................144

Resources...........................147

Photographic Information.....................149

Acknowledgements 151

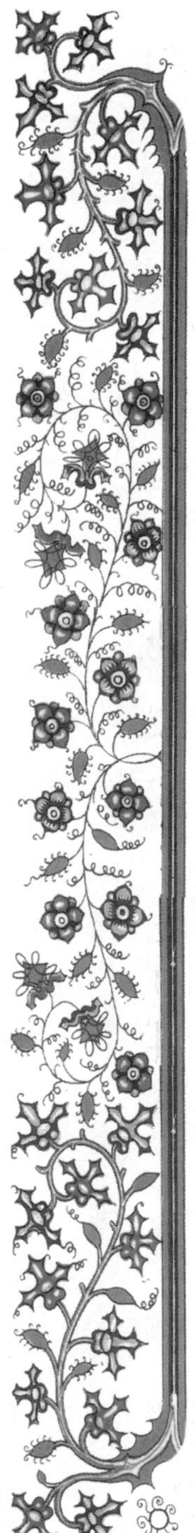

January

1

New Year's Day

2

1492: The Spanish army takes the city of Granada, Spain, from the Moors.

3

1521: Martin Luther excommunicated for speaking his mind.

4

1066: England's King Edward the Confessor dies.
1642: Sir Issac Newton, discoverer of the laws of gravity, born.

5

1589: Catherine d'Medici dies.

6

Twelfth Night / Epiphany
1412: Martyr Joan of Arc born.
1540: Henry VIII marries Anne of Cleves, his fourth wife.

7

1536: Catherine of Aragon, Henry VIII's first wife, dies.

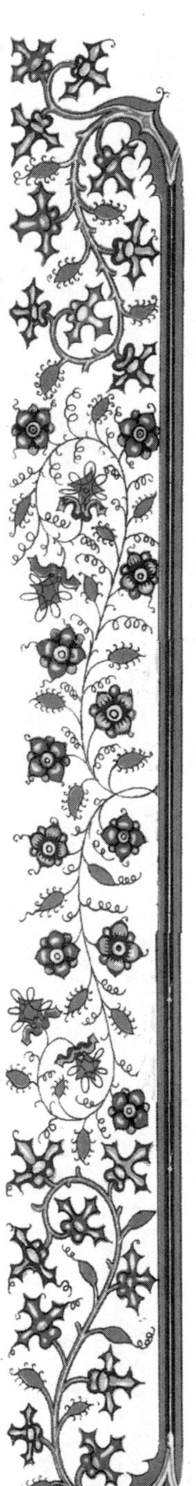

January

8

1499: Unicorn Tapestries made for the marriage of Anne of Brittany & Louis XII.

9

10

11

1569: Great Britain holds its first lottery on the steps of St. Paul's.

12

1582: Fernando Alvarez de Toledo, Duke of Alba, dies in Lisbon.

13

14

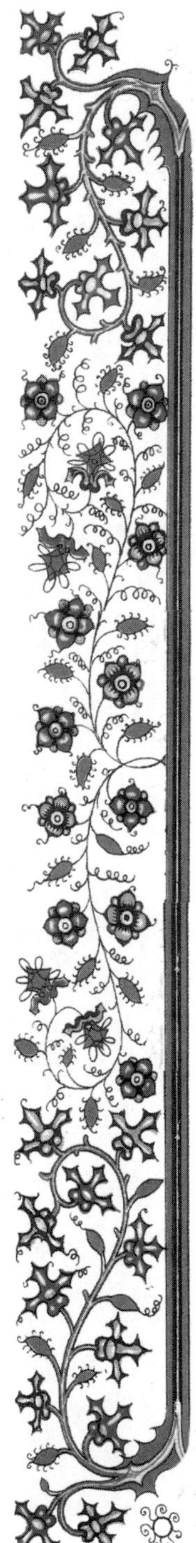

January

15

1559: Coronation of Queen Elizabeth I.

16

1599: Edmund Spenser, author of *The Fairie Queene*, dies.

17

1549: Sir Thomas Seymour arrested for treason against Elizabeth I.

18

19

1472: Astronomer Nicholas Copernicus born.

20

St. Sebastian's Day

21

St. Agnes' Day

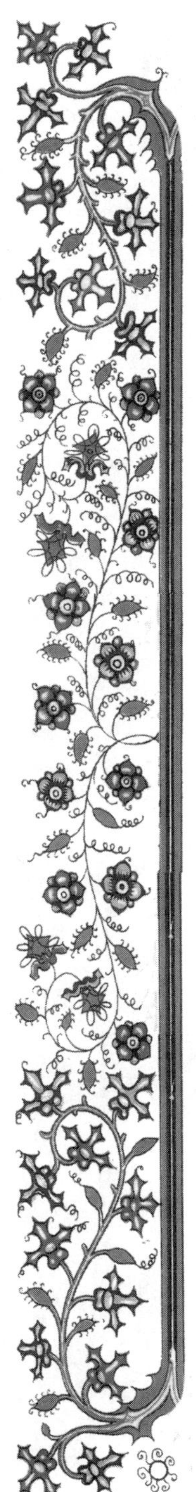

January

22

1561: Sir Francis Bacon born.

23

1542: King Henry VIII takes the title of King of Ireland.

24

1571: Queen Elizabeth opens the Royal Exchange, the first shopping mall.

25

St. Paul's Day
1533: Henry VIII marries second wife, Ann Boleyn.
1554: Thomas Wyatt's Rebellion.

26

27

28

1547: King Henry VIII dies; Edward VI becomes King of England.
1596: English explorer Sir Francis Drake dies.

Nicole Frugé

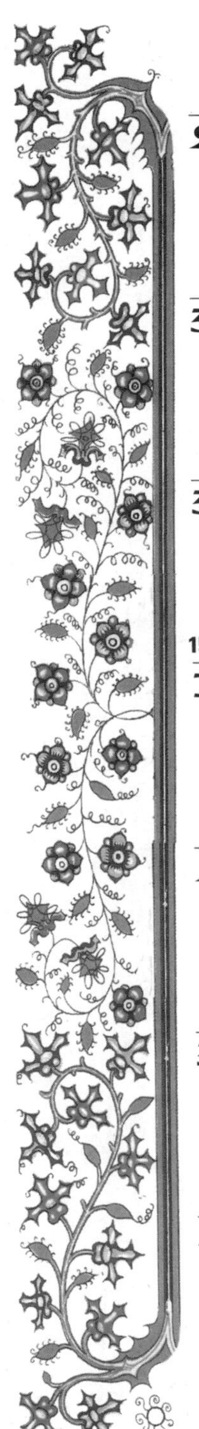

January/February

29

30

1649: Oliver Cromwell has Charles I executed at Whitehall.

31

1591: Dr. Fian of the North Berwick Witches found guilty & executed for witchcraft.

1

Imbolc, *Feast of the Goddess of Fertility*

St. Bridgid's Day, *patron saint of Irish nuns and dairy workers*

2

1587: Queen Elizabeth I has Mary, Queen of Scots, beheaded.

3

1468: Johannes Gutenberg, inventor of the printing press, dies.

4

Allen DeRico

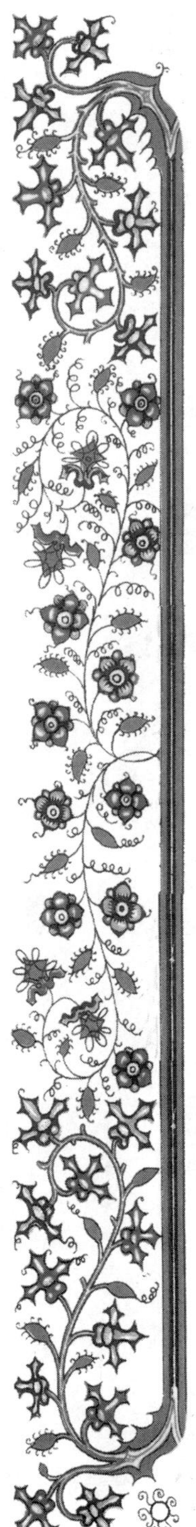

February

5

St. Agatha's Day

6

1564: Playright Christopher Marlowe born.

7

1274: St. Thomas Aquinas, scholar and philosopher, dies.
1478: Sir Thomas Moore born.

8

9

St. Appolonia's Day

10

1567: Lord Darnley, husband to Mary, Queen of Scots, murdered, perhaps even by Mary herself.

11

1254: British Parliament first convenes to discuss raising money for the military.
1531: Henry VIII recognized as the supreme head of the Church of England.

John Perry

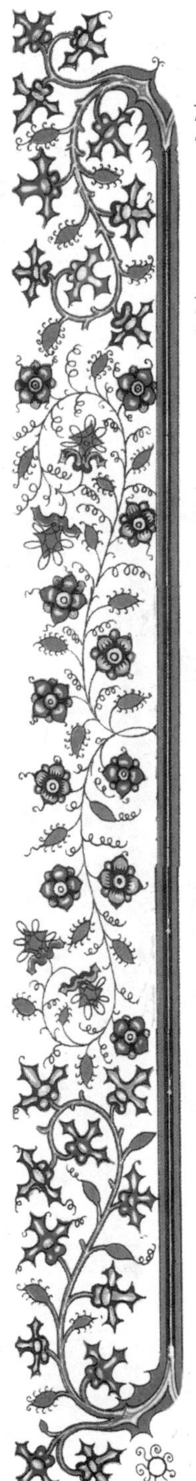

February

12

1554: Elizabeth I imprisoned in the Tower of London; Lady Jane Grey executed.

13

1542: Catherine Howard, Henry VIII's fifth wife, executed.
1633: Galileo detained by the Inquisition in Rome.

14

St. Valentine's Day

15

1564: Galileo Galilei born.

16

17

18

1516: Mary I, Queen of England, born.

Lady Kimberly

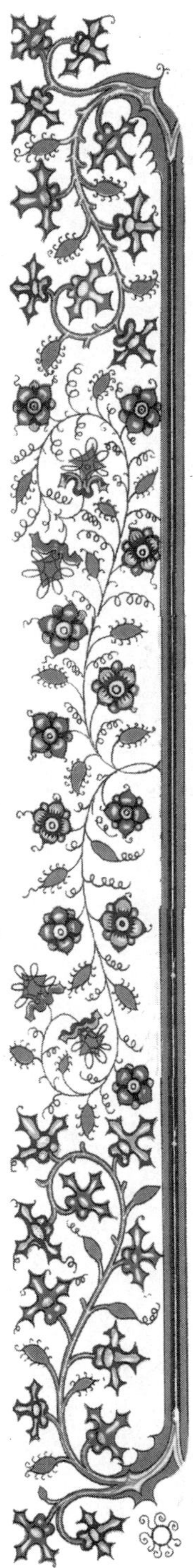

February

19

1473: Astronomer Nicolas Copernicus born.
1592: The Rose Theater opens in London.

20

1547: Edward VI crowned King of England at the age of nine.
1437: King James I of Scotland assassinated by his grandson, Robert, and others.

21

1599: Shareholders sign lease to build Globe Theatre in London.

22

1512: Explorer Amerigo Vespucci dies from malaria.

23

1555: Sir Thomas Wyatt beheaded for leading a rebellion against the crown.

24

1500: Charles V of Spain born.

25

1570: Queen Elizabeth I excommunicated by Pope Pius V, who proclaims that her own subjects are free to murder her without condemnation.
1601: Robert Devereux, Earl of Essex and favorite of Queen Elizabeth, executed.

Museum Replicas, Ltd.

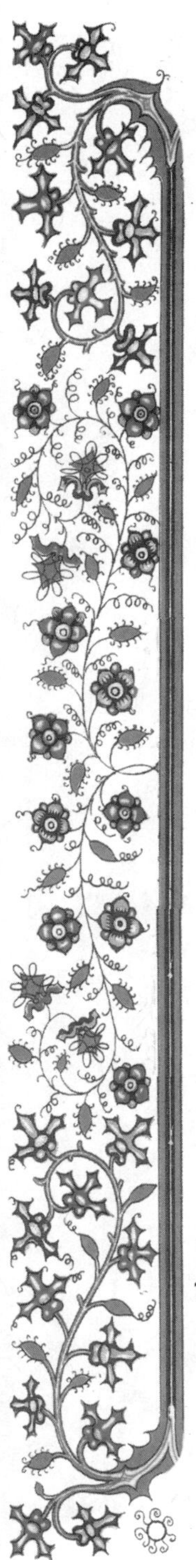

February/March

26

27

28

29

1

St. David's Day, *patron saint of Wales and poets*
Whuppity Scorie Day, Scottish festival of noisemaking to drive away evil spirits

2

St. Benedict's Day, *patriarch of western monks*
1966: Lady Kimberly of Sherburne Isle, Chronicler of *Renaissance Magazine*, born.

3

Simplicity Pattern Co.

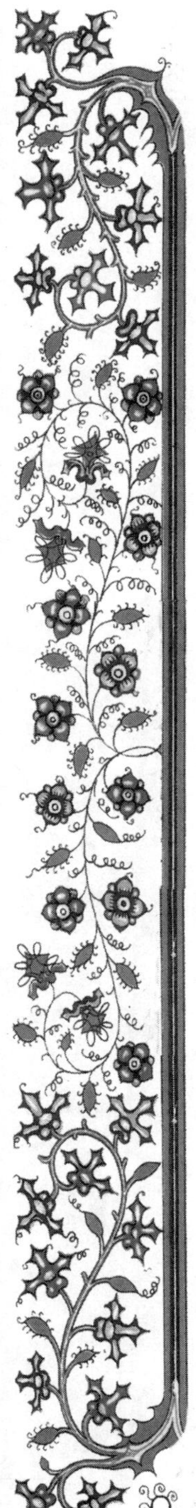

March

4

5

St. Piran's Day, *patron saint of Cornwall*

6

1475: Artist Michelangelo Buonarroti born.

7

St. Thomas Aquinas' Day

8

9

1401: Amerigo Vespucci, the navigator after whom America is named, born.

10

March

11

1302: Romeo and Juliet's wedding day, according to Shakespeare.

12

1559: Queen Elizabeth I makes peace with France.

13

14

15

Beware, the Ides of March!

16

1534: Henry VIII's England severs relations with the Church.

17

St. Patrick's Day, *patron saint of Ireland*
1328: Scotland wins its independence from England, ending 32 years of war.

Sterling, NY, Renaissance Festival

March

18

1314: Jacques de Molay, Grand Master of the Knights Templar, burned at the stake for heresy.

19

1549: Thomas Seymour executed.

20

Ostara / Spring Equinox

21

1556: England's Archbishop Thomas Cranmer burned at the stake.

22

23

24

1603: Elizabeth I dies, passing the throne to James VI of Scotland, thus joining England and Scotland under one rule.

Allen DeRico

March

25

1199: Pope Innocent III issues bull to establish the Inquisition.
1330: William Sinclair takes Robert the Bruce's heart on crusade.

26

27

1306: Robert the Bruce crowned King of Scotland at Scone.

28

29

30

31

1492: Ferdinand and Isabella sign an edict expelling the Jews from Spain.
1596: Mathematician and philosopher Rene Descartes born.

Simplicity Pattern Co.

April

1

All Fool's Day

1587: Sir Francis Drake sets sail from England to attack the Spanish fleet.

2

1513: Ponce de Leon, in pursuit of the Fountain of Youth, lands in Florida.

3

4

5

6

1199: King Richard "the Lionhearted" of England, dies.

7

Lady Kimberly

April

8

9

1105: Reprimanded by the Church for his long hair, England's King Henry I begrudgingly allows the bishop to shear his locks after Easter service.

10

11

12

1606: Great Britain adopts the Union Jack, which combines the Scottish cross of St. Andrew with the British cross of St. George.

13

1533: Anne Boleyn publicly declared Queen of England.
1598: King Henry IV of France signs the Edict of Nantes, granting civil rights to Protestant Hugenots.

14

1536: Wales becomes a part of England.

Nicole Frugé

April

15

1452: Artist, inventor Leonardo da Vinci born.

16

1570: Guy Fawkes born.

17

1194: Richard the Lionheart returns to England to be crowned a second time.
1542: Giovanni da Verrazano discovers New York Harbor.

18

19

20

1096: People's Crusade begins.
1534: The Maid of Kent, Eliza Barton, executed.

21

Lady Kimberly

April

22

1500: Pedro Alvarez Cabral discovers Brazil, claiming it for Portugal.
1509: Henry VIII crowned king of England.

23

St. George's Day; *proper to wear blue*
1350: Order of the Garter established by Edward III.
1564: William Shakespeare born.
1616: William Shakespeare dies.

24

1558: Mary, Queen of Scots, marries Francis, Dauphin of France.

25

1599: Oliver Cromwell born.

26

27

28

1603: Elizabeth I buried at Westminster Abbey.

Simplicity Pattern Co.

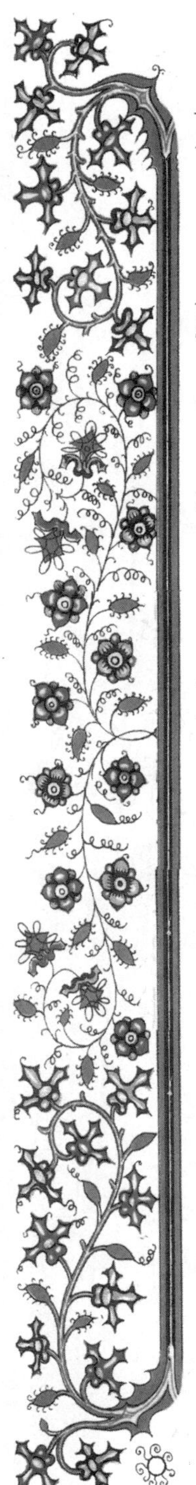

April/May

29

30

Beltane, *a night of supernatural occurrences*

1

May Day / Vernal Equinox
1169: First Normans land in Ireland.

2

3

1469: Niccolo Machiavelli, author of *The Prince,* born.

4

5

Simplicity Pattern Co.,

May

6

1541: Henry VIII proclaims that a new English Bible must be placed in every church.

7

St. Stanislaus' Day

8

1559: Act of Uniformity signed by Queen Elizabeth.

9

10

11

12

TXDOT

May

13

14

15

1567: Mary, Queen of Scots, marries James Hepburn, the Earl of Bothwell.

16

1587: Villagers of St. Julien, France, institute legal proceedings against vine weevils.

17

1536: Marriage of Henry VIII and Anne Boleyn declared null and void.

18

19

St. Ive's Day, *patron saint of Brittany and lawyers*
1536: Anne Boleyn beheaded for being a witch by Henry VIII.
1602: Martha's Vineyard, USA, first sighted by Captain Bartholomew Gosnold.

Museum Replicas. Ltd.

20

St. Bernardino of Siena's Day

21

1553: Lady Jane Grey marries Guilford Dudley.

22

23

1533: Marriage of King Henry VIII and Catherine of Aragon declared invalid by Archbishop Thomas Cranmer.

24

1543: Nicholas Copernicus dies.

25

26

The Image Group, Thomas M. Krekow, Kansas City, MO

May/June

27

St. Bede the Venerable's Day

28

29

1453: Constantinople falls to the Ottoman Turks, giving them a permanent foothold in Europe.

30

1431: Joan of Arc burned at the stake.
1536: Henry VIII marries Jane Seymour, his third wife.

31

1043: Lady Godiva rides naked through the market square in Coventry, England, in order to force her husband to lower the villagers' taxes.

1

1533: Anne Boleyn crowned Queen of England.
1593: Playwright Christopher Marlowe dies.

2

June

3

4

5

6

7

1329: Scotland's King Robert the Bruce dies.
1494: Spain and Portugal sign the Treaty of Tordesillas, dividing the New World between them.

8

Corpus Christi Day

9

St. Columba's Day, Abbot of Iona and patron saint of Ireland.

Lady Kimberly

June

10

St. Margaret of Scotland's Day

11

1509: Henry VIII marries Catherine of Aragon, his first wife.

12

1298: William Wallace routs the English at the Battle of Black Ironsides.

13

1398: Prince Henry Sinclair sets foot on American soil.

14

St. Basil the Great's Day

15

1215: Magna Carta signed by King John on the Isle of Runnymede.
1520: Pope issues bull condemning Martin Luther's works.
1606: Artist Rembrandt van Rijn born.

16

1329: The Black Prince—Edward, Prince of Wales—born.
1497: Amerigo Vespucci lands in the "New World."

Museum Replicas, Ltd.

17

18

19

1566: James I of England (and James VI of Scotland) born.

20

1484: The Pied Piper of Hamelin
spirits away 130 children, never to be seen again.

21

Litha / St. John's Eve / Midsummer's Eve / Summer Solstice

22

1559: Queen Elizabeth's Prayer Book issued.
1509: Catherine of Aragon crowned Queen of England.

23

1314: Scotland defeats England in the Battle of Bannockburn.
1603: James I of England outlaws pirateering.

The Image Group, Thomas M. Krekow, Kansas City, MO

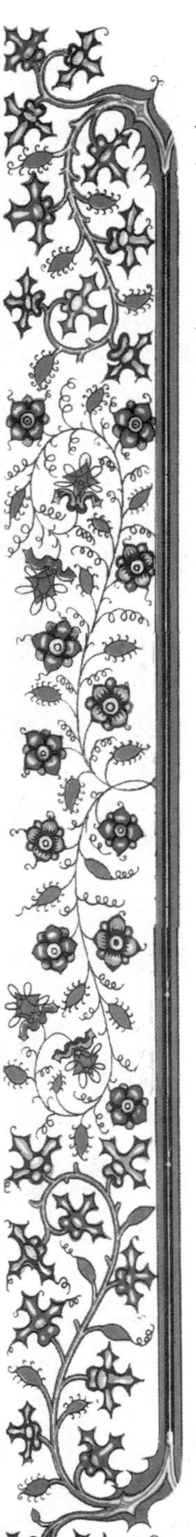

June

24

1497: John Cabot claims North America for England.
1509: Henry VIII crowned King of England.
1519: Infamous Lucrezia Borgia dies.

25

1580: The Book of Concord, a collection of doctrinal standards of the Lutheran Church, first published.

26

1541: Francisco Pizarro, Spanish conqueror of Peru, assassinated in Lima.

27

1462: Louis XII, King of France, born.
1550: Charles IX, King of France, born.

28

1098: The Crusaders defeat the Turks at Antioch, during the First Crusade.
1491: Henry VIII of England born.
1577: Flemish painter Peter Paul Rubens born.

29

1613: London's Globe Theatre burned down during first performance of Shakespeare's *Henry VIII.*

30

1470: Charles VIII, King of France, born.
1572: Great Britain's Poor Law passed, giving aid to the poor or work to the willing and able.

TXDOT

July

1

1536: England's Henry VIII's children Mary and Elizabeth declared illegitimate by Parliament.
1543: England and Scotland sign the Peace of Greenwich.

2

1489: Thomas Cranmer born.
1566: French astrologer, physician, and visionary Nostradamus dies.

3

4

1190: Richard I of England and Phillip II of France start out on the Third Crusade.

5

6

1189: King Henry II of England—the first of the Plantagenets—dies.
1553: England's Edward VI dies and is succeeded by Queen Mary I.

7

1307: Edward "Hammer of the Scots," dies enroute to quell the Scottish Rebellion.
1535: Sir Thomas More beheaded by Henry VIII for saying that the king could not rule both Church and State.

Catherine Summers, Sunshine Photography

July

8

1497: Vasco de Gama leaves Lisbon in search of a sea route to India.
1540: Henry VIII abolishes all books containing errors and heresy.

9

1540: The marriage of Anne of Cleves and Henry VIII dissolved.
1553: Lady Jane Grey proclaimed Queen of England.

10

1099: Spanish warrior-hero "El Cid" dies.
1509: John Calvin, founder of the Puritan ideal, born.

11

1274: Scotland's Robert the Bruce born.
1533: Pope Clement VII excommunicates England's King Henry VIII.
1564: The Black Plague arrives in Stratford, England.

12

1191: In the Third Crusade, Richard the Lionheart takes the city of Acre.
1543: Henry VIII marries Katherine Parr, his sixth and final wife.

13

14

St. Bonaventure's Day, Cardinal-Bishop of Albano
1223: Philip II, King of France, dies.

Museum Replicas, Ltd.

July

15

1099: Crusaders capture Jerusalem, restoring the Holy City to Christendom.
1606: Artist Rembrandt Harmenszoon van Rijn born.

16

1048: Bendict IX, the "Boy Pope," resigns from the Papacy.
1557: England's Anne of Cleves dies.

17

1453: The Battle of Castillon, end of the Hundred Years' War.

18

1536: Authority of the Pope declared void in England by an act of Parliament.
1610: Italian painter Caravaggio dies.

19

St. Vincent de Paul's Day
1333: Edward III of England defeated by the Scots at the Battle of Halidon Hill.
1588: Spanish Armada sighted off the Cornish coast of England.

20

1304: Lyric poet Petrarch born.
1553: Lady Jane Grey deposed and Mary Tudor proclaimed Queen of England.

21

1403: Henry "Hotspur," (aka Henry Percy), killed in battle at Shrewsbury.
1542: To fight against Protestantism, Pope Paul III sets up an Inquisition.

The Image Group, Thomas M. Krekow, Kansas City, MO

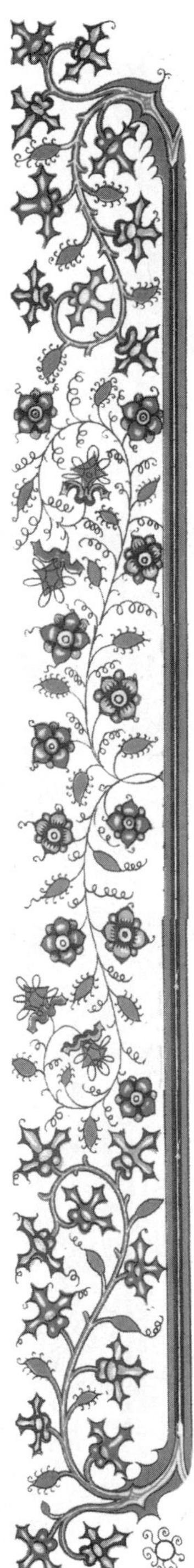

July

22

St. Mary Magdalene's Day

1298: English annihilate Sir William Wallace's forces at the Battle of Falkirk.

1587: English settlers arrive on Roanoke Island, VA.

23

24

1567: Mary, Queen of Scots, forced to abdicate throne by the English; James VI declared King of Scotland at the age of one.

25

St. James' Day and St. Christopher's Day

1554: England's Queen Mary I and Spain's King Philip II marry at Winchester.

26

St. Anne's Day, *patron saint of housewives*

27

1540: Thomas Cromwell, advisor to King Henry VIII, executed for treason.

28

1540: England's King Henry VIII marries Catherine Howard, his fifth wife.

1586: First potatoes arrive in England from New World.

Dennis Cline

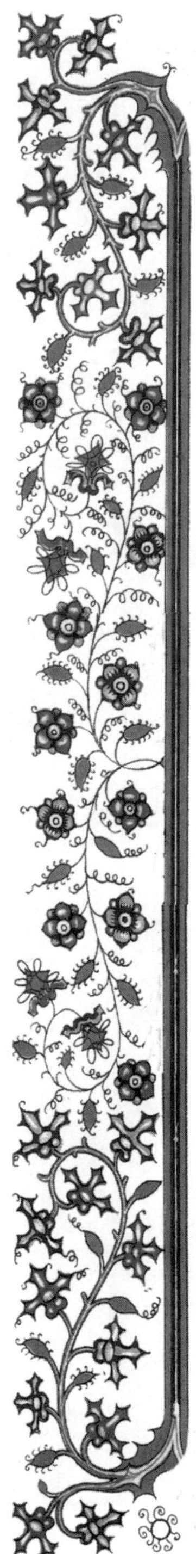

July/August

29

1099: Battle of Ascalon—the final battle of the First Crusade, fought.
1565: Mary, Queen of Scots, marries her cousin, Lord Darnley.
1588: Sir Francis Drake and the British fleet rout the Spanish Armada.

30

31

1556: St. Ignatius of Loyola, founder of the Jesuits, dies.

1

Lammas, *beginning of 30-day agrarian festival*
1291: The Republic of Switzerland founded.

2

1578: Juliet Capulet born, according to Shakespeare.
1589: Jacques Clement assassinates King Henry III of France.

3

1460: James II of Scotland killed by the English during seige of Roxburgh Castle.
1492: Christopher Colombus sets sail from Spain in search of a trade route to India.

4

St. Dominic's Day
1060: Henry I of France dies.

Museum Replicas, Ltd.

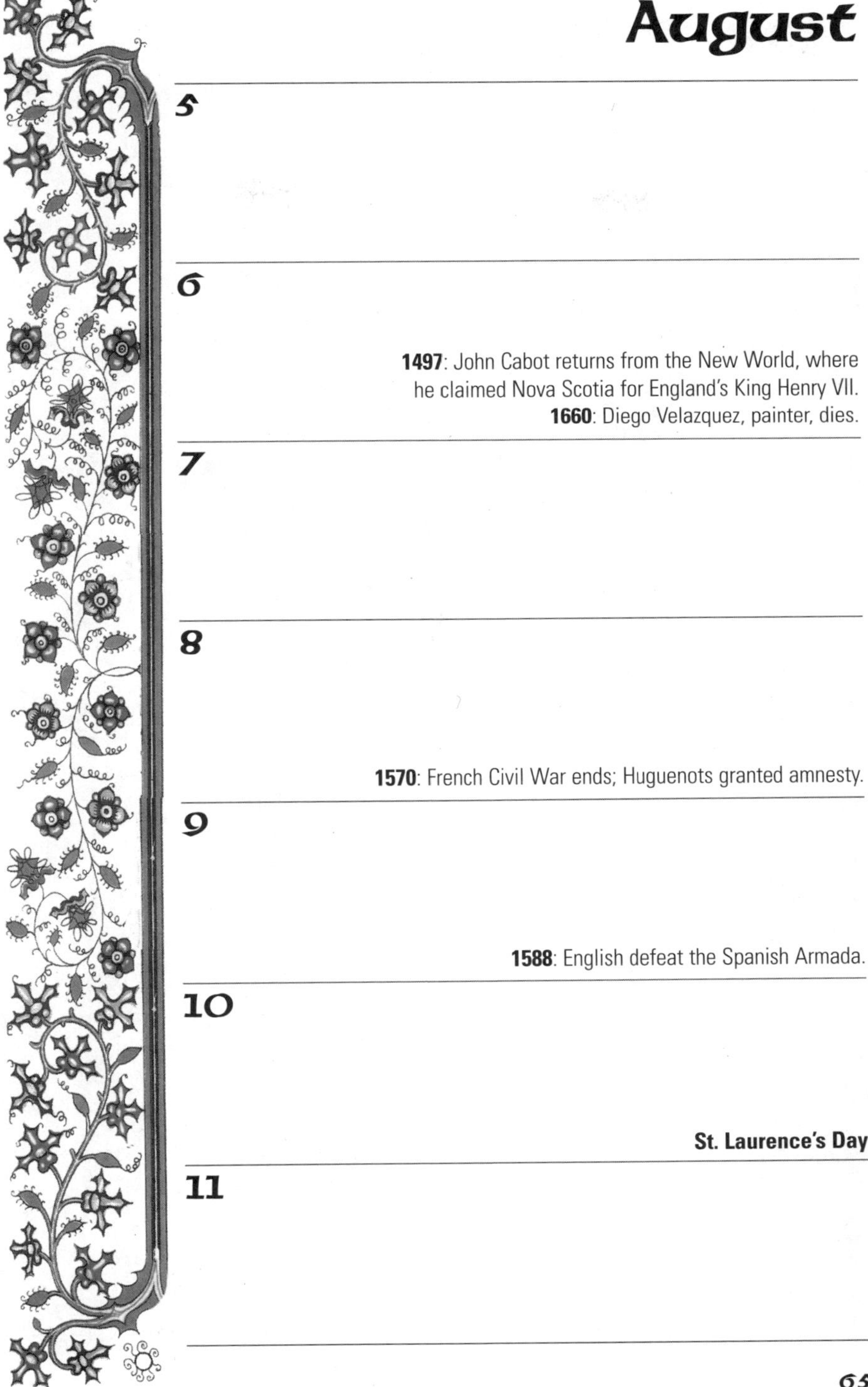

August

5

6

1497: John Cabot returns from the New World, where he claimed Nova Scotia for England's King Henry VII.
1660: Diego Velazquez, painter, dies.

7

8

1570: French Civil War ends; Huguenots granted amnesty.

9

1588: English defeat the Spanish Armada.

10

St. Laurence's Day

11

Lady Kimberly

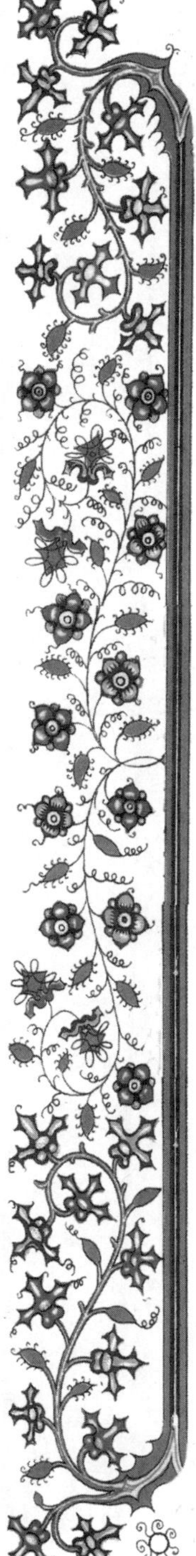

August

12

1099: Crusaders defeat the Egyptians at Ascalon.
1503: Christian III, King of Denmark and Norway, born.
1530: Florence restored to the Medicis after a siege of 10 months.

13

St. Cassian's Day *patron saint of school teachers*
1521: Hernán Cortés captures and destroys Tenochtitlán (Mexico City).
1624: Louis XIII appoints Cardinal Richelieu, chief minister of France.

14

1040: Duncan I killed in battle by Macbeth, his only rival to the Scottish throne.

15

1057: Macbeth killed by Malcolm Canmore near Aberdeen, Scotland.
1534: The Jesuit Order founded in Paris by St. Ignatius of Loyola.

16

1513: England's King Henry VIII defeats the French at the Battle of the Spurs.

17

St. Rock's Day
1585: Spanish forces led by the Duke of Parma take Antwerp during the Dutch War of Liberation.

18

1587: Virginia Dare, first child born to English parents in the New World, born.

The Image Group, Thomas M. Krekow, Kansas City, MO

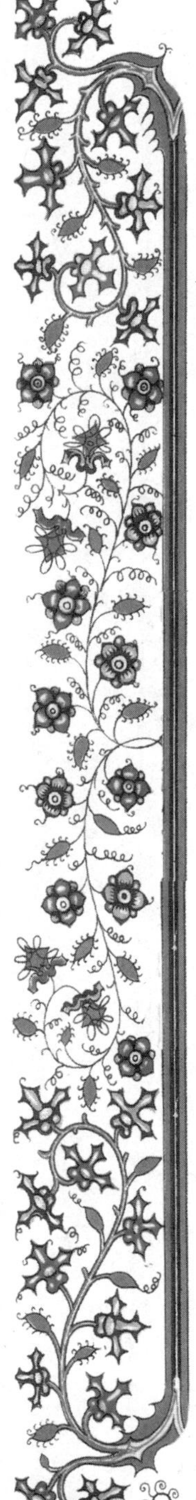

August

19

1477: Maximilian I succeeds Frederick III as Holy Roman Emperor.
1561: Mary, Queen of Scots, arrives in Scotland to assume the throne, after spending 13 years in France.

20

St. Bernard's Day, *abbot of Clairvaux*

21

1165: Philip II, King of France, born.

22

1485: King Richard III slain at the Battle of Bosworth Field.
1623: Order of the Rosy Cross established in Paris.
1642: King Charles of England declares war on Parliament.

23

1305: Sir William Wallace hanged, drawn, and quartered in London.

24

St. Bartholomew's Day
1572: St. Bartholomew's Day massacre; 70,000 Huguenots killed in France.

25

1270: King Louis IX of France, leader of the Seventh Crusade, dies.
1530: Ivan the Terrible, Russian Tzar, born.

Dennis Cline

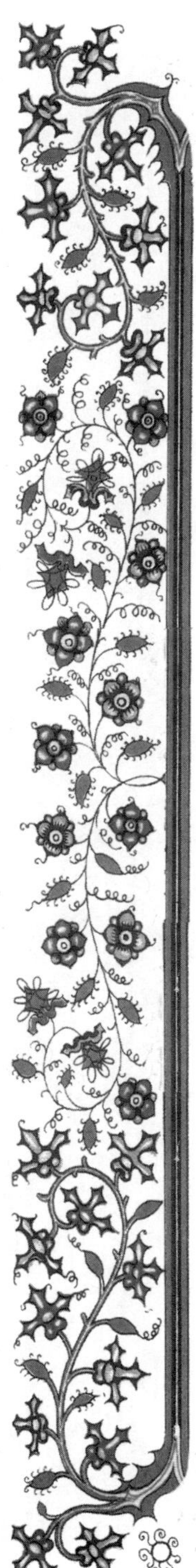

August/September

26

1346: English forces defeat the French at the Battle of Crecy.

27

1576: Venetian painter, Titian, dies.

28

St. Augustine's Day, *bishop of Hippo*
1619: Ferdinand II elected Holy Roman Emperor.

29

1350: English defeat the Spanish fleet at the Battle of Winchelsea.

30

St. Rose of Lima's Day
1483: Louis XI of France dies and is succeeded by his son, Charles VIII.

31

1422: England's King Henry V dies of dysentery in France and is succeeded by his 9-month-old son, Henry VI.

1

St. Giles' Day
1159: Pope Adrian IV dies, the only Englishman to be elected Pope.

Allen DeRico

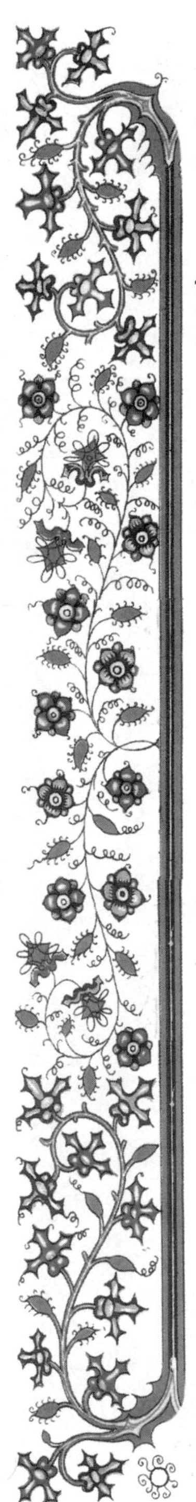

September

2

1666: The Great Fire of London started by Thomas Farrinor, baker to King Charles II.

3

1189: King Richard the Lionhearted crowned King of England.
1609: Henry Hudson discovers the island of Manhattan.

4

1483: Richard III supposedly orders the Princes in the Tower murdered.

5

1548: Katherine Parr, England's King Henry VIII's sixth wife, dies in childbirth.

6

1522: Juan Sebastian Del Cano completes first circumnavigation of the world.
1666: Great Fire of London ends.

7

1533: England's Queen Elizabeth I born.

8

1157: England's King Richard the Lionhearted born.
1565: Spanish establish first permanent European settlement in North America in St. Augustine, FL.

Lady Kimberly

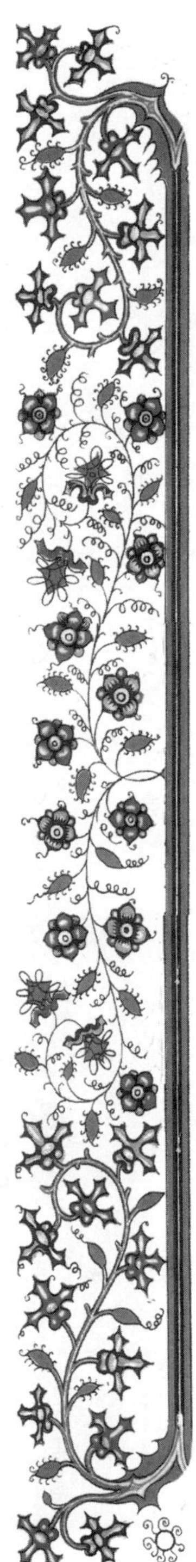

September

9

1087: William the Conqueror dies.
1513: Battle of Flodden, Scotland, at which James IV is killed.
1543: Mary, Queen of Scots crowned at age 9 months.

10

954: King Louis IV of France dies.

11

1297: Led by William Wallace, Scottish defeat British at the Battle of Sterling.
1649: Oliver Cromwell besieges Drogheda, massacring most of its inhabitants.

12

1494: Francis I, King of France, born.
1609: Henry Hudson enters the Hudson River in North America.

13

1598: King Philip II of Spain dies.

14

Holy Rood Day
1321: Dante Alighieri, author of *The Divine Comedy,* born.
1486: Cornelius Agrippa born.

15

Museum Replicas, Ltd.

September

16

1380: Charles V "the Wise" of France, dies.
1387: Henry V, king of England, born.
1498: Tomas de Torqemada, the first Grand Inquisitor of Spain, dies.

17

879: Charles II "the Simple" of France, born.

18

1502: Christopher Columbus lands in Costa Rica.
1544: Roman Emperor Charles V and Francis I of France sign Peace of Crespy, ending the last war between them.

19

1356: Edward III "The Black Prince" defeats King John II of France in the Battle of Poitiers.
1551: The last of the Valois monarchs—King Henry III of France—born.

20

1198: French defeat King Richard I at the Battle of Gisors.
1519: Ferdinand Magellan sets out from Spain to circumnavigate the globe.

21

St. Matthew the Apostle's Day
1327: King Edward II of England murdered in Berkeley Castle.

22

1499: The Swabian War ends, giving Switzerland its independence.
1515: Anne of Cleves, England's King Henry VIII's fourth wife, born.

Simplicity Pattern Co.

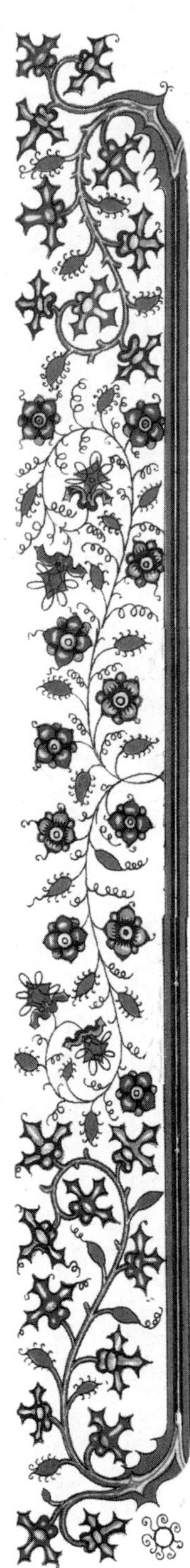

September

23

Mabon / Autumnal Equinox
1518: England's Royal College of Physicians established.

24

1143: Pope Innocent II dies.

25

1493: Columbus sets sail from Spain on his second voyage to the New World.
1513: Spanish explorer Vasco Nuñez de Balboa discovers the Pacific Ocean.

26

1580: Sir Francis Drake returns to England after taking his ship around the world in 33 months.

27

St. Cosmas and Damian's Day
1540: Pope Paul III approves the first outline of the Jesuit Order.

28

29

Michaelmas / Feast of St. Michael
1399: King Richard II resigns the English throne to Henry IV.

Allen DeRico

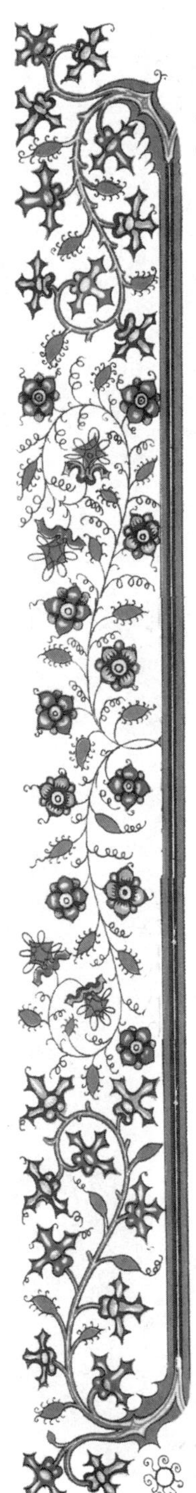

September/October

30

St. Jerome's Day

1

1537: England's Lady Jane Grey born.

2

1187: Saladin captures Jerusalem from the Christian Crusaders.
1452: England's King Richard III born.

3

St. Francis of Assisi's Day, *founder of the Franciscan Order*

4

1289: King Louis X "the Quarrelsome" of France, born.
1550: Charles IX of Sweden born.
1582: The last day of the Julian calendar in Spain and Portugal.

5

1285: King Philip III of France dies of plague and is succeeded by Philip IV "the Fair."

6

1536: Religious reformer William Tyndale is burned at the stake as a heretic.

The Image Group, Thomas M. Krekow, Kansas City, MO

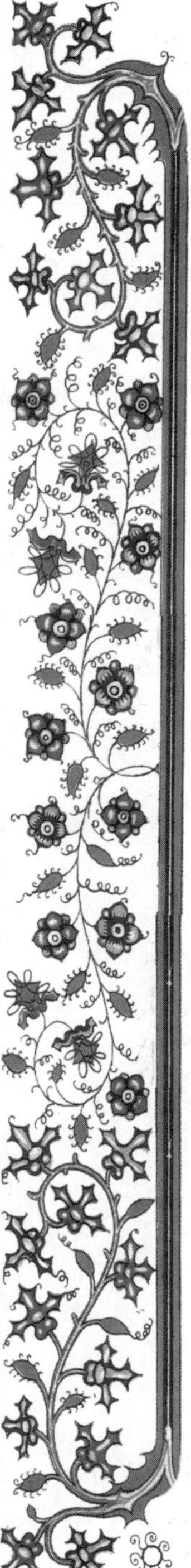

October

7

1571: Battle of Lepanto, the greatest sea battle in 600 years, fought between Austria and Turkey.

8

St. Bridget's Day

9

1000: Leif Erikson lands in North America.
1547: Author Michael Cervantes born.

10

732: Charles Martel defeats Saracens at the Battle of Poitiers.

11

1521: King Henry VIII presents a book denouncing Martin Luther's teachings to Pope Leo X, and in exchange is given the title "Defender of the Faith."

12

1492: Christoper Columbus lands in the Bahamas, believing he has found Asia.
1537: Edward VI born.

13

St. Edward the Confessor's Day
1307: Knights Templar arrested for heresy in France by King Phillip IV.

Museum Replicas, Ltd.

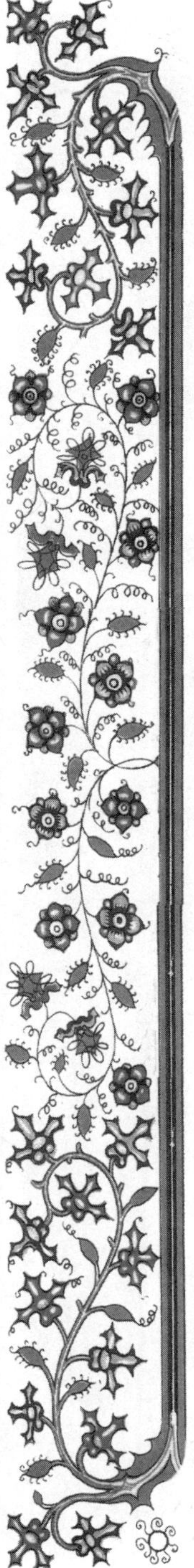

October

14

1066: William the Conqueror defeats King Harold at the Battle of Hastings.
1322: England forced to accept Scotland's independence after Robert the Bruce defeats the English at Byland, north of York.

15

1581: First major ballet, commissioned by Catherine d'Medici, staged in Paris.
1582: Gregorian calendar adopted by all Catholic countries, eliminating ten days from calendar; October 5 thus becomes October 15.

16

1430: Scottish King James II born.

17

18

St Luke the Evangelist's Day
1469: Isabella of Castille marries Ferdinand II of Aragon, uniting Spain.
1685: King Louis XIV of France revokes Edict of Nantes, depriving Protestant Huguenots of their civil liberties.

19

1216: King John of England dies.

20

1524: Thomas Linacre, first president of the Royal College of Physicians of London and physician to Kings Henry VII and VIII of England, dies.

Simplicity Pattern Co.

October

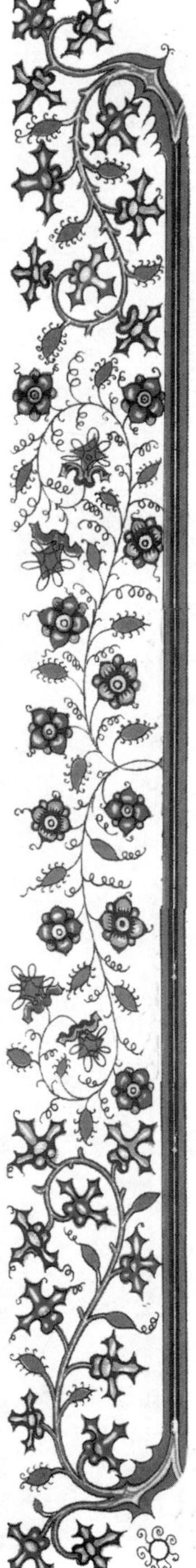

21

St. Ursula and her Maiden's Day

1422: Charles VI of France dies. His fits of insanity earned him the title "Charles the Mad."

22

23

24

St. Raphael the Archangel's Day

1537: Jane Seymour, England's King Henry VIII's third wife, dies.

25

1400: Geoffrey Chaucer, English poet and author of *The Canterbury Tales,* dies.

1415: England's Henry V defeats the French at the Battle of Agincourt, ending the Hundred Years' War.

26

899: Saxon King Alfred the Great of England dies.

1440: Gilles de Rais hanged after being accused of satanism and the murder of 140 children. His crimes inspired the tale of "Bluebeard."

27

Lady Kimberly

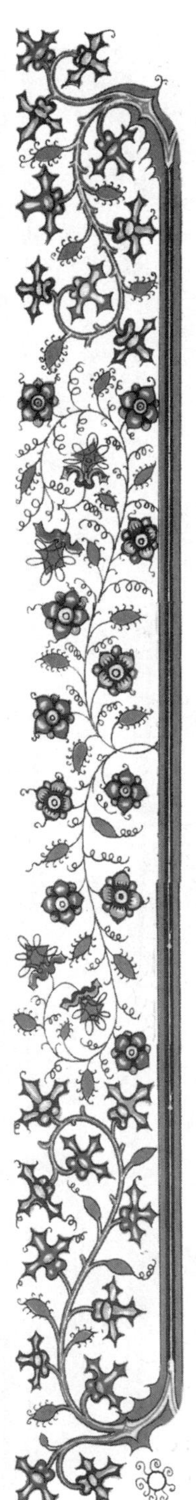

Oct./November

28

St. Simon and St. Jude the Apostle's Day

29

1618: Sir Walter Raleigh executed in London for treason.

30

1553: Mary I crowned Queen of England.

31

Samhain, Celtic New Year / All Hallows' Eve

1517: Martin Luther posts his 95 Theses on a door of the Castle Church in Wittenburg, Germany, beginning the Protestant Reformation.

1

All Souls' Day

1500: Benvenuto Cellini, Italian sculptor and goldsmith, born.

2

1483: Henry Stafford, Duke of Buckingham, beheaded for his rebellion against England's King Richard III.

3

St. Hubert's Day, *Bishop of Liege*

Museum Replicas, Ltd.

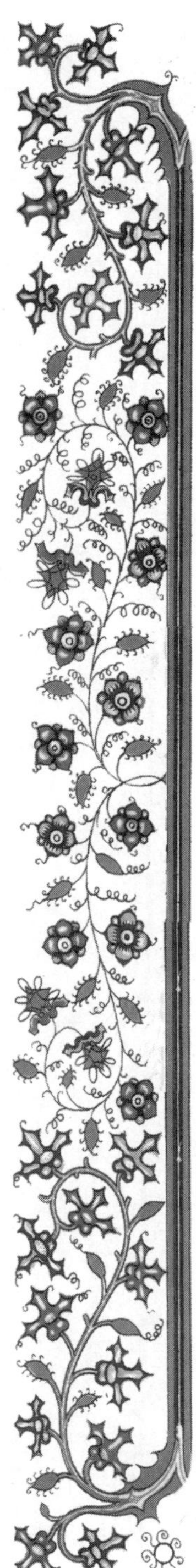

November

4

St. Charles Borromeo's Day, *Archbishop of Milan*

5

Guy Fawkes Day

1605: Guy Fawkes and other Catholic leaders attempt to blow up England's Protestant House of Lords.

6

1429: Henry VI crowned king of England.

7

8

9

10

1483: Religious leader Martin Luther born.

1567: Mary, Queen of Scots, abdicates her throne.

1567: Robert Devereaux, favorite of Elizabeth I, born.

Simplicity Pattern Co.

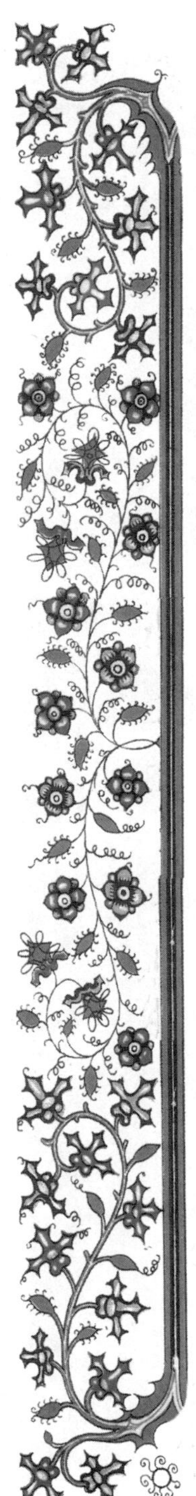

November

11

Samhain ends / Martinmas
1528: Margaret Hunt reveals the secrets of her medical practice of healing the sick before the Bishop of London.

12

1035: King Canute the Great of England, Denmark, and Norway, dies.

13

1312: Edward III of England born.

14

1533: Spanish forces under Francisco Pizzaro capture the Inca capital of Cusco.

15

1315: The Swiss defeat Leopold of Austria at the Battle of Morgarten.

16

1272: King Henry III of England dies.

17

Accession Day
1534: The Act of Supremacy passed, declaring England's King Henry VIII head of the Church of England.
1558: Elizabeth I ascends the British throne after the death of Mary I.

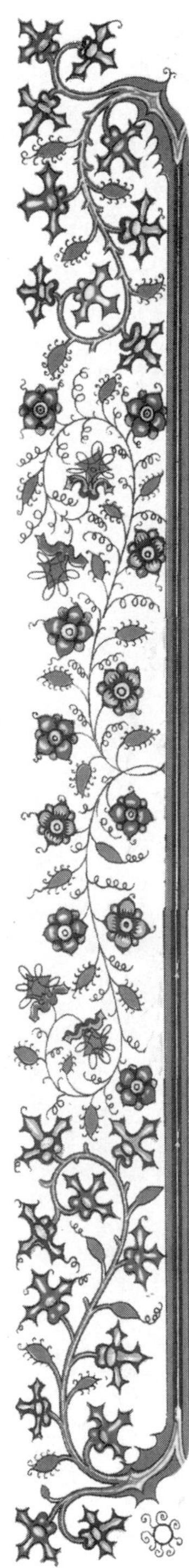

November

18

1189: William II, last Norman king of Sicily, dies.
1477: William Caxton publishes the first printed book in the English language.
1626: Rome's St. Peter's Basilica consecrated by Pope Urban VIII.

19

1600: Charles I, King of Scotland and England, born.

20

21

1306: Pope Clement issues bull to arrest the Knights Templar, confiscating their territories and property.

22

1497: Vasco de Gama becomes first explorer to round Cape of Good Hope.

23

1221: King Alfonso X "the Wise" of Castile and Leon, born.
1499: Imposter and pretender to the throne of England, Perkin Warbeck, executed.
1585: Composer and first writer of the Anglican liturgy, Thomas Tallis, dies.

24

Museum Replicas, Ltd.

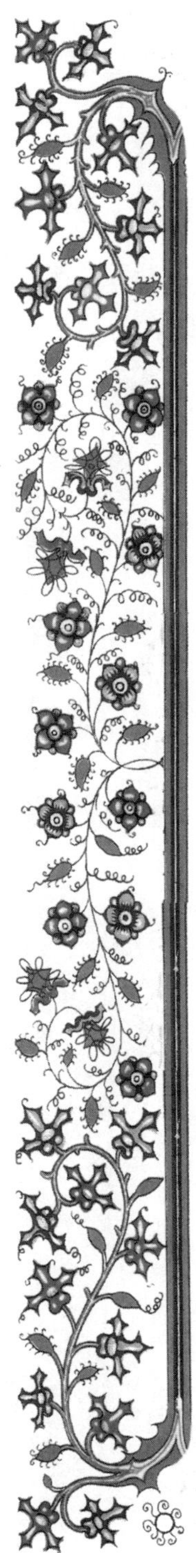

Nov./December

25

1488: Elizabeth I crowned Queen of England.

26

27

1095: Pope Urban II calls for the First Crusade.

28

1520: Ferdinand Magellan reaches the Pacific Ocean from the Atlantic.
1582: William Shakespeare marries Anne Hathaway.

29

1489: Margaret Tudor born.

30

St. Andrew's Day, *patron saint of Scotland*

1

St. Eligius' Day, *Bishop of Noyon*

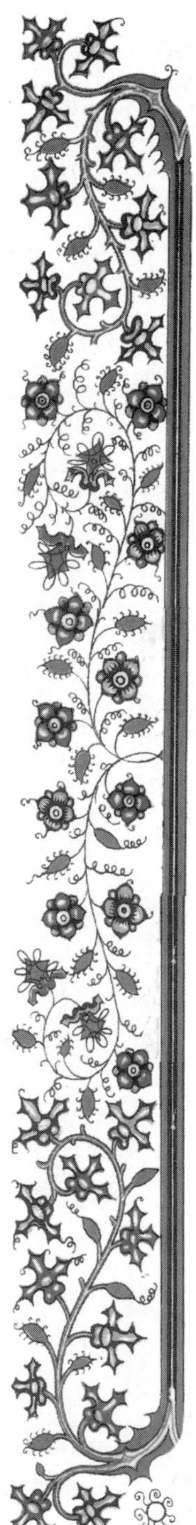

December

2

3

1621: Galileo perfects the telescope.

4

St. Barbara's Day

5

1560: King Francis II of France dies.

6

St. Nicholas' Day, *Bishop of Myra*

7

St. Ambrose's Day, *Bishop of Milan*

8

1524: Mary, Queen of Scots, born.

Museum Replicas, Ltd.

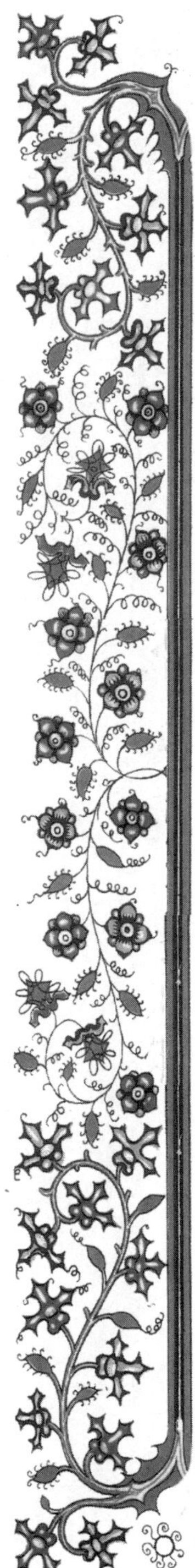

9

10

11

12

1531: The Virgin of Guadalupe appears to Juan Diego.

13

1258: Pope Alexander IV issues first Papal bull dealing with sorcery.
1577: Sir Francis Drake sets out to be the first to sail around the world.

14

1503: Healer, psychic Nostradamus born.
1542: James V of Scotland dies.

15

1485: Catherine of Aragon, King Henry VIII's first wife, dies.

Simplicity Pattern Co.

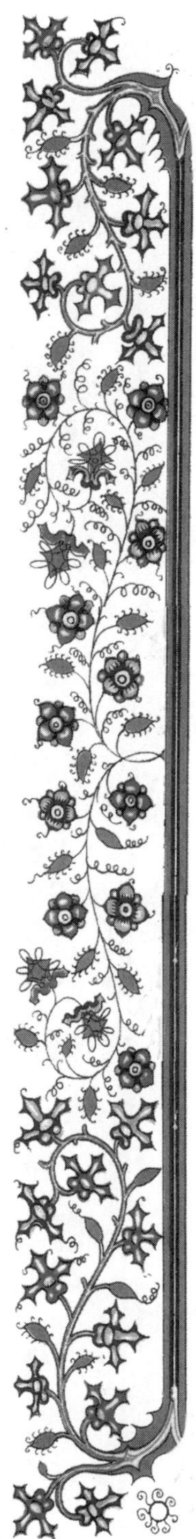

December

16

17

18

19

1547: Great Britain passes the vagabond law, to whip or brand those who refused to find gainful employment.

20

21

St. Thomas the Apostle's Day

22

Yule / Winter Solstice

Museum Replicas, Ltd.

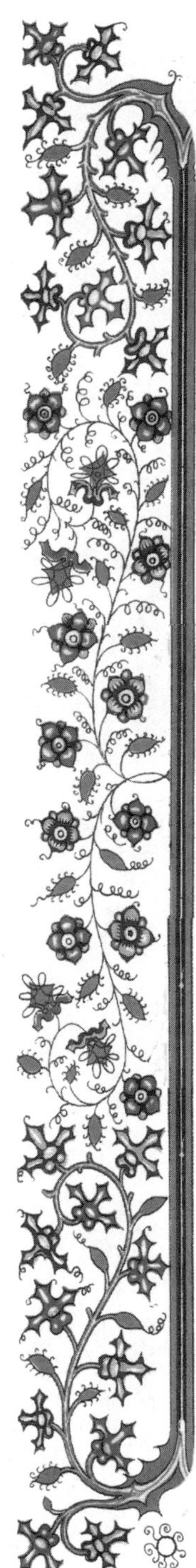

December

23

24

1515: Thomas Wolsey is appointed Chancellor of England by Henry VIII.

25

Christmas Day
1154: Pope Adrian IV enthroned, history's only British pope.

26

St. Stephen's Day, *the first martyr*
Boxing Day, *when gifts were originally to be given to the servants*

27

St. John the Evangelist's Day

28

29

St. Thomas á Becket's Day
1170: Archbishop Thomas á Becket assassinated in Canterbury cathedral.

Simplicity Pattern Co.

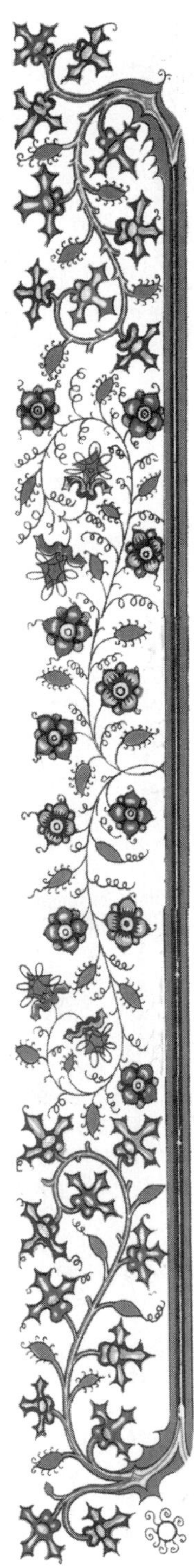

December/January

30

1546: England's King Henry VIII's will names Edward his heir.

31

Hogmanay / Cake Day / New Year's Eve

1

New Year's Day
1651: Charles II crowned King of Scotland.

2

3

St. Genevieve's Day

4

St. Elizabeth Ann Seton's Day

5

1066: Edward the Confessor dies.

A Dictionary of Medieval Terms

A

ABJURATION: A renunciation, under oath, of heresy to the Christian faith, made by a Christian wishing to be reconciled with the Church.

ACHIEVEMENT: A full display of armorial bearings.

AMERCEMENT: A financial penalty inflicted at the mercy of the king or his justices, for various minor offences. The offender is said to be "in mercy" and the monies paid to the crown to settle the matter is called "amercement."

APOSTATE: One who leaves a religious order which was considered a serious crime in the eyes of the Church, being not only a breach of faith with God but also with the founders and benefactors of their religious house.

ARGENT: The heraldic color (tincture) of silver/white.

ARMIGER: A person entitled to bear heraldic arms.

ARPENT: A measure of land roughly equal to a modern acre.

ASSART: To turn woodlands into pasture or cropland. To "assart" lands within a forest without a license was a grave offense.

ASSIZE: The meeting of feudal vassals with the king, or the decrees issued by the king after such meetings.

ASYLUM (Right of): The right for a Bishop to protect a fugitive from justice or to intercede on his behalf. Once asylum was granted, the fugitive could not be removed for one month's time. Fugitives who found asylum had to pledge an oath of abjuration never to return to the realm, after which they were free to find passage out of the realm. If found within the borders after a month's time, they could be hunted down as before, with no right of asylum to be granted ever again.

B

BALDRIC: A silk sash or leather band slung over one shoulder and round the opposite hip. In medieval times it was decorated by silver or gold bells. Later it was fastened on the left hip and carried the sword holder.

BAN: A King's power to command or prohibit any action, under pain of punishment or death, usually because of a break in the "King's Peace." Also a royal proclamation, either of a call to arms or a decree of outlawry. In clerical terms, a ban was an excommunication or condemnation by the church.

BANALITIES: Fees which a feudal lord imposed on his serfs for the use of his mill, oven, wine press, or similar facilities. It sometimes included part of a fish catch or the proceeds from a rabbit warren.

BARBER-SURGEON: A monastic who shaved faces/heads and performed light surgery.

BARBETTE (also Gorget): A piece of white linen pinned to a woman's hair at each side of the head and draped around the chin and in front of the neck. Survives in nun's attire. Worn in the 13th and 14th centuries.

BARBICAN: The gateway or outerworks defending the drawbridge to a castle.

BARD: A minstrel or poet who glorified the virtues of the people and his chieftains.

BARON: A vassal who served as a member of the king's great council. It was not, of itself, a title, but rather a description of the Tenants-in-Chief class of

nobility.

BARONET: Originally English Barons who had lost the right of their individual summons to Parliament. Often these titles were sold to gentlemen willing to set up plantations in Ireland or Nova Scotia.

BASTION: A small tower located either at the end of a castle's curtain wall or in the middle of the outside wall.

BATTLEMENT (also Crenelation): A narrow wall built along the outer edge of a castle's wall walk to protect the soldiers from attack.

BEGUIN (also Flemish Hood): A rectangle of linen carefully folded into a symmetrical headdress and caught together at the nape of the neck.

BENEFICE: A grant of land given to a member of the aristocracy, a Bishop, or a monastery, for limited or hereditary use, in exchange for services. In ecclesiastic terms, a benefice was a church office that returned revenue.

BENEFIT OF CLERGY: A privilege enjoyed by members of the clergy, placing them beyond the jurisdiction of secular courts.

BERM: The flat space between the base of the curtain wall and the inner edge of the moat.

BIGGIN: A cap men wore to bed which tied under the chin with laces or ribbon.

BLACK MONKS: A common name for members of the Benedictine Order, derived from the color of their habits.

BLAZON: The technical language for the written description of armorial bearings.

BLIAUD: An over-tunic worn by both sexes in the early Middle Ages. It was fairly long and belted at the waist, while the skirt was often slit at the sides or in front to allow easier movement. A knee-length bliaud was worn by both peasants and soldiers.

BOMBAST: Padding made of cotton and rags used to stuff in the linings of 16th-century garments.

BONGRACE (1530-1615): A flat, square cap with a short flap of velvet on each side.

BOROUGH: A town granted the right of self-government, by royal charter.

BRAIES: Loose drawers or breeches belted or tied with cord at the waist, the lower end tucked into the hose below the knee. After the 13th century, braies become shorter in the leg as the hose grew longer and, by the later 15th century, became short underpants.

BREHON LAWS (also *Feinechus*): An ancient Gaelic legal system.

BUM-BARREL (also Bum-Roller, Waist Bolster): A padded roll tied around the waist and worn under the skirt, to hold it out.

BURGESS: The holder of land or a house within a borough.

CANIONS (1570-1620): Tubular, thigh-hugging extensions worn from breeches to knee. Separate "netherstocks" could be gartered either over or under them.

CANTING ARMS: A coat of arms where the "charge" is a pun on the owner's name.

CASSOCK (1530-1660): Worn by men and women, this was a loose, hip-length coat with a small collar or hood.

CAUL: A skull cap of silk, worn alone or under a hat, often worn by maidens, or a bag-shaped hair net (of gold mesh lined with silk, or made entirely of silk thread with human hair), which held the hair back in a coil.

CHAINSE: A white long-sleeved undertunic of fine linen worn in the early Middle Ages. In feminine costume it was ground-length. Later it developed into the shirt and the chemise.

CHAMBERLAIN: An officer of the royal household responsible for the Chamber, meaning that he controled access to the person of the king. He was also responsible for administration of the household

and the private estates of the king. The Chamberlain was one of the four main officers of the court, the others being the Chancellor, the Justiciar, and the Treasurer.

CHANCELLOR: The officer of the royal household who served as the monarch's secretary or notary. The Chancellor was responsible for the Chancery, the arm of the royal government dealing with domestic and foreign affairs. Usually the person filling this office was a Bishop chosen for his knowledge of the law.

CHANSONS DE GESTE: Literally "songs of deeds," they were epic poems composed by troubadours and sung by jongleurs to audiences gathered at the halls of nobles, or in public places.

CHARGE: The generic term for pictorial representations that can be placed on various parts of a shield (such as animals, plants, or objects).

CHARTER OF FRANCHISE: Documents granting liberty to a serf by his lord, or the freedom of servitude to feudal lords, granted to the inhabitants of a town or borough.

CINQUEFOIL: A stylized flower with five radiating petals or leaves, used in heraldry.

CODPIECE (or Braguette): Originally an inverted triangular section of cloth sewn into the hose around a man's groin, the codpiece by the 16th century was padded and boned and became so large that it was often used to carry small weapons, jewels, or food (hence the reference to a man's genetalia as the "family jewels.")

CONSTABLE: An officer who commanded an army or an important garrison, or the officer who commanded in the king's absence.

COTEHARDIE: A term used extensively for both feminine gowns and masculine tunics from 1300 until 1430. It is generally applied to fitting garments, buttoned part- or full-length, and having long or half sleeves.

COTTAGER: A peasant of lower class who owned a cottage, but owned little or no land.

COUNT: The continental equivalent of the English Earl, ranked second only to a Duke.

CRESPIN (or Creppin): A fine, linen cap.

CREST: A generic term for the ornaments mounted on helmets.

CROSS-GARTERING: Strips of linen wound round the braies to hold them in position.

CULDEES: Meaning "servant of God," they were Irish/Scottish preservers of old Gaelic customs.

CURTAIN WALL: The high wall that surrounded the inner ward, or the open area in the center of a castle.

D

DAUB: A mud and clay mixture applied over wattle to strengthen and seal it.

DEMESNE: The part of the lord's manorial lands reserved for his own use and not allocated to his serfs or freeholder tenants. Serfs worked the demesne for a specified numbers of days a week.

DENARIUS: The English silver penny, hence the abbreviation "d."

DEXTER: The right-hand side of a shield.

DIMIDIATION: In heraldry, the method of impalement in which the dexter half of one coat of arms was joined to the sinister half of the other.

DIOCESE: A district subject to the jurisdiction of a Bishop/Archbishop. The name was derived from the administrative districts created by the Roman emperor Diocletian.

DOUBLET: A masculine tunic worn especially from the 15th to 17th century. Originally of quilted manufacture, although its style changed over the years, it remained a fundamental outer body garment.

DUKE: From the Roman *Dux*, a Duke ruled a district called a *duchy*. In England, the title was reserved for members of the royal family.

DUN: A Scottish single-family hill fort.

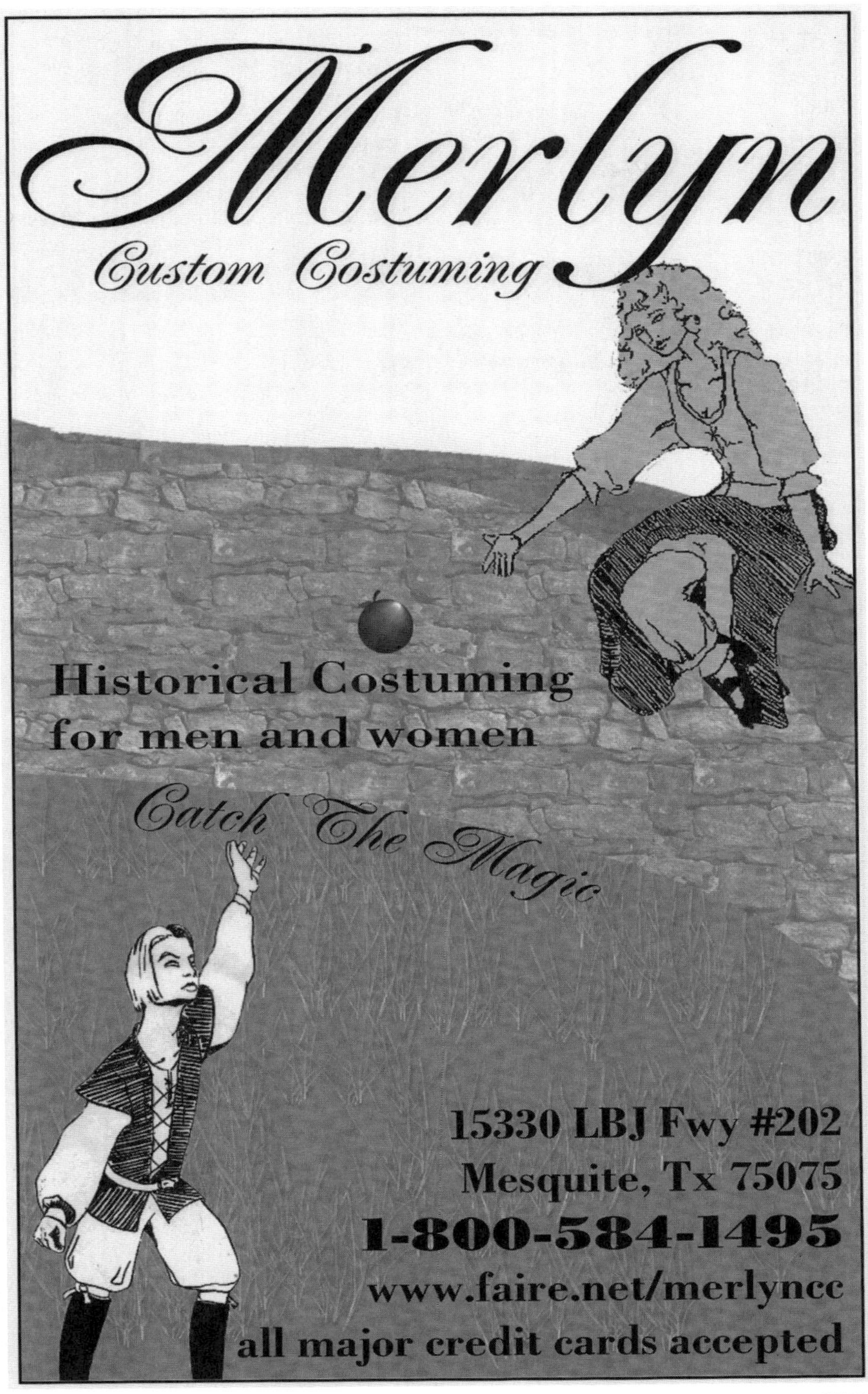
Merlyn
Custom Costuming
Historical Costuming
for men and women
Catch The Magic
15330 LBJ Fwy #202
Mesquite, Tx 75075
1-800-584-1495
www.faire.net/merlyncc
all major credit cards accepted

E

EARL: The highest title attainable by an English nobleman who was not of royal blood. Alsc known in earlier times as *Ealdorman.*

EIRE: Ireland.

EMBRASURE: The low segment of the alternating high and low segments of a battlement.

ESCHEAT: The right of a feudal lord to the return of lands held by his vassal, or the holding of a serf's land, should he either die without lawful heirs or suffer outlawry.

ESCUTCHEON: A small charge in the form of a shield.

EXCHEQUER: The financial department of the royal government. The chief officers of the Exchequer were the Treasurer, the Chancellor, and the Justiciar. Sheriffs, in their role as regional chief accountants, presented reports to the Exchequer at Easter and Michaelmas.

EYRE: The right of the king (or justices acting in his name) to visit and inspect the holdings of any vassal, usually done at intervals of a few years.

F

FAIR: A market held at regular intervals, usually once to twice a year. Fairs tend to offer a wider range of goods than normal markets and were generally licensed by either the king, a local lord, or a chartered town.

FALLING BAND (also Falling Collar) (1540-1670): Any turned-down collar, often lace-edged, and worn instead of a ruff.

FARM: A fixed sum or rent, usually paid annually, for the right to collect all revenues from land. Lords could "farm" land to vassals, receiving a fixed annual rent in place of the normal feudal obligation. Many sheriffs "farmed" out their shires, contracting in advance to pay a fixed annual sum to the crown, thus obtaining the right to collect any additional royal revenues for their own profit.

FARTHINGALE: The canvas or linen petticoat containing whalebone hoops worn in the 16th century.

FEALTY (Oath of): The oath by which a vassal swore loyalty to his lord, usually on a religious relic or on the Bible.

FEUDALISM: The system of governing whereby semiautonomous landed nobility had certain responsibilities to the king, in return for the use of grants of land (fiefs), worked by the labor of a semi-free peasantry (serfs).

FIEF: Heritable lands held under feudal tenure, or the lands of a Tenant-in-Chief. Often called a Holding.

FIELD: In heraldry, the surface of a shield on which charges are placed.

FOREPART: Any underskirt—usually highly decorated—which was revealed through the inverted-V opening in the front of a skirt.

FORMARRIAGE (also Merchet): The sum commonly paid by a serf to his lord when the serf's daughter married a man from another manor.

FRANK PLEDGE: The legal condition under which each male member of a tithing (district) over the age of 12 was responsible for the good conduct of all other members of the tithing.

FRENCH HOOD (1530-1630): A small bonnet made on a stiff frame and worn far back on the head. Folds of material fell below the shoulders from a short flat panel at the back. They were usually dark in color but decorated with "biliments" (borders of silk, satin, or velvet, and trimmed with gold or jewels) and worn over a crespin.

FYRD: The Anglo-Saxon militia. Special "King's Peace" prevailed while journeying to, from, or during Fyrd service.

G

GABARDINE: A long, loose overcoat with hanging sleeves, worn by both sexes and of all classes.

GAEL: A name given to Celtic inhabitants of Scotland, Ireland, and the Isle of Mann.

PLUS... AN INTERVIEW WITH RITCHIE BLACKMORE OF BLACKMORE'S NIGHT!
Renaissance
AN INTERVIEW WITH
Cate Blanchett
OF ELIZABETH
The Courtships of
Queen Elizabeth
LADIES' MEDIEVAL
COURTESY BOOKS
JOAN OF ARC
Behind the Scenes
of the Joan of Arc
A Most
Honorable
Gazette...
500 Years
in the
Making.
Yes, I wish to subscribe!
Name
Street
City/State/Zip
❑ 1-Year Subscription (4 issues): $17 . . . .
❑ 2-Year Subscription (8 issues): $32 . . . .
❑ 3-Year Subscription (8 issues): $45 . . . .
Overseas Shipping Fee: . . . .
Total Enclosed: . . . .
Method of Compensation
❑ Check or money order ❑ Visa ❑ MasterCard
Card #
Expiration Date
Signature
Mail order form and make checks payable to Renaissance Magazine, 13 Appleton Road, Nantucket, MA 02554.
Canadian and overseas orders, add $6 per year for extra shipping costs.

GALLIGASKINS (also Slops): Wide, loose breeches.

GARDE-CORPS: A 14th-century garment which evolved from the surcoat, which was either sleeveless or had elbow-length wide sleeves.

GARDEROBE: A small latrine or toilet built into the thickness of a castle's wall.

GUILD: Trade associations formed to protect members from the competition of foreign merchants and to maintain commercial standards. Guild apprentices served a master for five to seven years, before becoming a journeyman at about age 19. Journeymen worked in the shop of a master until they could demonstrate that they were ready for master status. Guild members were forbidden to compete with each other, and merchants were required to sell at a just price.

GULES: The heraldic color (tincture) of red.

H

HALF-TIMBER: The common form of medieval construction in which walls were made of a wood frame structure, filled with wattle and daub.

HANSEATIC LEAGUE: An association of merchants and towns in northern Germany.

HERIOT: A payment which a feudal lord could claim from the possessions of a dead serf or other tenant; essentially a death tax. Generally, however, if a tenant died in battle, the heriot was forgiven.

HIDE: A unit of measurement for assessment of tax, approximately 120 acres (although it may have varied between 60 and 240 acres), or the amount of land that could be cultivated by an eight-ox plow in one year.

HOARDING: A temporary wooden balcony suspended from the tops of walls and towers and erected before a battle, from which missiles and arrows could be dropped or fired.

HOMAGE: The ceremony by which a vassal pledged fealty to his liege and acknowledged all of his other feudal obligations, in return for a grant of land.

HONOR: A holding, or group of holdings, forming a large estate, such as the land held by an Earl.

HOUPPELANDE: A full over-gown worn by both sexes chiefly from 1375 to 1424. Earlier examples had high collars with wide sleeves and were ground-length.

HOWDEN: A college of secular priests.

HUE AND CRY: The requirement of all members of a village to pursue a criminal with horn and voice.

I

IMPALED: In heraldy, describes a shield divided per "pale" to incorporate the arms of two different families, side by side.

INTERDICT: The ecclesiastical banning of all sacraments—except for baptism and extreme unction and for sacrements performed on high feast days. Interdicts were enforced to force persons, institutions, a community, or a secular lord to accept a view dictated by the Church or Pope.

J

JERKIN (1545-1575, 1620-1630): A sleeveless vest of cloth or leather worn over the doublet.

JONGLEUR: French wandering minstrels (which included musicians, acrobats, jugglers, and clowns), usually from the lower class, who entertained with tales of epic battles and heroes.

JUS PRIMAE NOCTIS *(First Night)*: The right by which a lord could sleep with the bride of a newly married serf on the first night of their marriage, although the custom could be avoided by the payment of a fine.

JUSTICIAR: The head of the royal judicial system and the king's viceroy, when the actual viceroy was absent from the country.

K

KNIGHT: The retainer of a feudal lord who owed military service for his fief. The ideals to which a knight could aspire were notably prowess, loyalty, generosity, and courtesy.

KNIGHT'S FEE: In theory, a fief which provided sufficient revenue to equip and support one knight, which was approximately 12 hides or 1,500 acres (although the term applies more to revenue a fief could generate than its size).

L

LEASE FOR THREE LIVES: A term of lease of land usually for the life of its holder, his son or wife, and a grandson.

LIRIPIPE: The lengthened peak of the medieval hood.

M

MAN-AT-ARMS (also Yeoman): A soldier holding his land, generally 60 to 120 acres, in exchange for military service.

MANDILION (also Manderville) (1520-1560, 1577-1620): A loose, thigh-length overcoat with a standing collar and loose sleeves.

MANOR: A small holding, typically from 1,200 to 1,800 acres, with its own court and probably its own hall, but not necessarily having a manor house. The manor as a unit of land was generally held by a knight (knight's fee) or managed by a bailiff for some other holder.

MARCHER LORDS: The name commonly given to Norman landholders on the Welsh border.

MARK: A measure of silver, generally eight ounces. In England, a mark was worth 13 shillings and four pence, or two thirds of one pound.

MARQUESS (or Marquis): Lords responsible for guarding border areas, known as "marches." In some cases, the eldest son of a Duke was known as a Marquess.

MARY STUART HOOD (1550-1630): Similar to a French hood but made of a sheer cloth, trimmed with decorative fabric, and edged with lace. The front border had a V- or U-shaped curve above the middle of the forehead.

MEAD: A wine made of fermented honey.

METHEGLIN: Spiced or medicated mead, popular in Wales.

MINSTREL: A poet and singer who lived and traveled off the largess of the aristocracy.

MONEYER: A person licensed by the crown to strike coins. He received the dies from the crown and was allowed to keep 1/240 of the money coined for himself.

MONMOUTH CAP (1570-1625): A knitted wool cap that fit the head, and had a brim and a long peaked top that hung over one side and ended in a tassel. Common especially among soldiers and sailors.

N

NIGHT RAIL: A garment in which some wealthy women slept. Sleeping in the nude or in a shift was more common, however.

O

OR: The heraldic color (tincture) of gold, or yellow.

ORDEAL: A trial in which the accused was given a physical test (usually painful and/or dangerous) which could only be met successfully if he was innocent.

P

PALATINATE: In England, a county in which the Tenant-in-Chief exercised powers, normally reserved for the king, including the exclusive right to appoint a Justiciar, hold courts of Chancery and Exchequer, and to coin money.

PALE: In heraldry, a charge in the form of a broad vertical band in the center of the shield.

VON NUREMBERG
GERMANY

PALISADE: A sturdy wooden fence usually built to enclose a site until a permanent stone wall could be constructed.

PANTOFFLE: In the 16th century, this was an overshoe which was slipped on top of the shoe or hose and had no back. Later the word was used for slippers.

PARTICOLORING: A medieval system of decoration wherein one half or one quarter of a garment was in one color and design and the other(s) were of a different one.

PATTEN: A wood, leather, or cork undersole which was fastened on the foot by straps and buckles and worn out-of-doors to protect the hose and soft shoes.

PEASECOD-BELLY: The unusual masculine silhouette produced by padding the doublet front to give a paunch shape. The fashion spread from Spain and was especially extreme in France.

PEERAGE: Hereditary titles (such as Count, Duke, and Earl), often linked to lands, powers, or responsibilties. For instance, English and Scottish peers had the right of summons to parliament.

PERRY: A liquour made from pears.

PICADILS: The scalloped or tabbed edge at the neck and armhole, fashionable in late 16th and early 17th-century dress. The name "Piccadilly" was given to this London thoroughfare because of a tailor there who specialized in making picadils.

PIPKIN (1565-1595): A taffeta hat trimmed with ostrich feathers and decorated with jewels. It had a moderate crown, a narrow, fairly flat brim, and was worn over a caul.

PLASTRON: An armor metal breastplate or the fur front of the sideless surcoat worn by medieval ladies.

POMANDER: From the French *pomme d'ambre*, a hollow, perforated sphere containing a waxed perfumed ball impregnated with scent, such as ambergris, musk, cloves, or hartshorn. Men wore pomanders suspended from a chain; women attached them to their girdles. Especially fashionable in the 16th century.

PORTCULLIS: A heavy timber grille that could be raised or lowered between the towers of each gate house.

POSTERN GATE: A side, or less important gate, into a castle.

POULAINE: The style of footwear which had an extended or exaggerated length at the toes. As the fashion was said to be most extreme in Poland, the English versions were termed "Krackows" after the Polish city of that name.

POURPOINT: The medieval body garment or tunic which later became the doublet.

PRIMOGENITURE: The right of the eldest son to inherit the estate or office of his father.

PRIORY: Any religious house administered by a prior or prioress. If the prior was subject to a resident abbot, the house was called an abbey or monastery.

PURPURE: The heraldic color (tincture) of purple.

R

RAMPANT: In heraldry, describes quadrupeds (often a lion) shown erect, one back paw raised, looking to the dexter.

REBATO (1580-1635): Of Spanish origin, a collar or ruff wired to stand up around a low-necked bodice.

REBUS: A heraldic device that is a pictorial pun on the name of the bearer.

REEVE: A royal or manor official appointed by the lord or elected by the peasants.

RELIEF: The fee paid by the heir of a deceased person on securing possession of a fief. Tradition determined the amount demanded.

RUFF (1550-1630): A circular collar in the form of a starched and crimped or pleated frill. From 1562 to 1577, ruffs measured about three inches wide and two inches deep, becoming separate articles of clothing by 1570. The cartwheel ruff was in fashion from 1550 to 1610 and the fan-shaped ruff, made

almost entirely of lace, from 1570 to 1625. Men's ruffs were generally higher in back than in front, following the line of the jaw, to frame the face and set off the shape of the skull.

S

SABLE: The heraldic color (tincture) of black.

SALTIRE: A charge in the form of a St. Andrew's cross.

SCUTAGE: The sum that the holder of a knight's fee would pay his lord in lieu of military service. Sometimes used as a form of tax.

SERF: A semi-free peasant (cottagers, small holders, or villeins) who worked his lord's demesne and paid him certain dues in return for the use of land, the possession (not ownership) of which was heritable. These dues ("corvee"), were in the form of labor on the lord's land, averaging three days a week.

SERGEANT: A servant who accompanied his lord to battle, a horseman of lower status used as light cavalry, or a type of tenure in service of a non-knightly character who might have carried the lord's banner, served in the wine cellar, or made bows and arrows. Sergeants paid the feudal dues of wardship, marriage, and relief, but were exempt from scutage.

SHERIFF (from "Shire Reeve"): The chief administrative and judicial officer of a shire. He collected taxes and forwarded them on to the Exchequer, and was also responsible for making sure that the King's table was well stocked.

SIEGE: The military tactic that involved the surrounding and isolation of a castle, town, or army, by another army, until the trapped forces were starved into surrender.

SIMONY: The buying or selling of spiritual things, particularly Church offices and benefices.

SINISTER: In heraldry, designates the left-hand side of the shield, or the right for the spectator.

SLOP-HOSE: Sailor's breeches.

SMALL HOLDER: A middle class peasant, farming more land than a cottager but less than a villein. A typical small holder would have farmed 10 to 20 acres.

SNUFKIN (also Snoskyn): A muff made of cloth or fur, the smaller models of which hung suspended from a woman's girdle.

STEWARD: The man responsible for running the day-to-day affairs of the castle when the lord was absent.

STOMACHER: A separate front panel of rich decorative fabric which ended in a point at the waist and was worn on top of the bodice.

SULONG: A measurement of land equal to two hides.

SWISH-WASH: A liquour made with honey and water and spiced with a dash of pepper.

T

TABARD: A sleeveless or short-sleeved tunic worn over armor in the Middle Ages. Where appropriate, arms decorated the garment, making it a coat-of-arms.

TALLAGE: A tax levied on boroughs and on the tenants living on royal estates, to help liquidate royal debts.

TENANT-IN-CHIEF: A lord or institution (the Church being most common) holding land directly from the king. All Earls were Tenants-in-Chief.

THANE: Originally meaning a Military Companion to the King, a thane was a man holding administrative office.

TINCTURE: The generic term for the heraldic metals, colors, and furs.

TIPPET: Name given to the streamers hanging from the elbow-length sleeves of the medieval tunic or gown. Also, a short shoulder cape for women.

TITHE: One tenth of a person's income given to support the church annually.

TONSURE: The rite of shaving the crown of the head of a person joining a monastic order or the secular clergy, symbolizing admission to the clerical state.

TOWN AIR IS FREE AIR: Words used in town charters to proclaim freedom of any serf who lived there for a year and a day, without being claimed by his lord.

TREASURER: The chief financial officer of the realm and senior officer of the Exchequer.

TROUBADOUR: Composers of epic poems, such as the *Chansons de Geste,* and love songs, often sung by wandering minstrels.

TRUNK HOSE (1540-1625): A style of breeches for men who wanted to show off their legs. Trunk hose consisted of a padded ring from the waist around the hips, to which long netherstocks were sewn.

TURRET: A small tower rising above and resting on one of the main towers of a castle, usually used as a look-out point.

U

USURY: Interest charged on a loan; a practice forbidden by Church law.

V

VASSAL: A free man who held land (fief) from a lord to whom he paid homage and swore fealty. He owed various services and obligations, primarily military, but he also advised his lord and paid him the traditional feudal aids required on the knighting of the lord's eldest son, the marriage of the lord's eldest daughter, and the ransoming of the lord, should he be held captive.

VENETIANS: Breeches fastened at the knee and separate from the netherstocks, distended with vertical rolls of padding down the inside of each side seam. A codpiece was not worn with Venetians, which buttoned or tied in a concealed front opening.

VERT: The heraldic color (tincture) of green.

VILLEIN: The wealthiest class of peasant, they usually cultivated 20-40 acres of land, often in isolated strips.

VIRGATE: One quarter of a hide.

VISCOUNT: The fourth level of peerage, a viscount was a lieutenant or deputy of a count (from "vice-count"), or the title of courtesy for the eldest son of an Earl or Marquess.

W

WAISTCOAT (1485-1625): An optional male undergarment, usually quilted, to which the breeches were fastened. A woman's dressing jacket was also called a waistcoat.

WALL WALK: The area along the top of a castle's walls from which soldiers defended both castle and town.

WARDSHIP: The right of a feudal lord to the income of a fief during the minority of its heir. The lord was required to maintain the fief and to take care of the material needs of the ward. When the ward came of age, the lord was required to release the fief to him in the same condition in which it was received.

WATTLE: A mat of woven sticks and weeds.

WIMPLE: A simple headcovering worn by women. A piece of material, square or circular in shape, was draped over the head to the shoulders and held in place by a band around the brow. Later a wimple was worn with a barbette or chin band so that the throat and chin were also covered.

Fashions
for the
Elizabethan
Look
Gift Certificates
Catalogue
Bridal Kits
"Diana"
Unicorn Clothing Companuy
924 San Andres Santa Barbara CA 93101
805.962.7048 phone/fax www.unicornclothing.com

Renaissance Faire Contacts

ALABAMA

Renaissance Faire
One weekend in October
Bill Warren
P.O. Box 431
Florence, AL 35631
(256) 766-3234

Alabama Shakespeare Festival and Renaissance Faire
One weekend in June
Thomas Stephens
1 Festival Dr.
Montgomery, AL 36117
(334) 271-5346
asftour@mindspring.com
www.asf.net

ALASKA

Three Barons Renaissance Fair
Two weekends in June
Carol LaLone
PO Box 233617
Anchorage, AK 99523
(907) 274-2913

ARIZONA

Arizona Renaissance Festival
February-March
Jeffrey Siegel
12601 East Highway 60
Apache Junction, AZ 85219
(520) 463-2600

Devonshire Renaissance Festival
One weekend in September
Art Molina
Los Olivos Senior Center
2802 E. Devonshire
Phoenix, AZ 85016
(602) 256-3130

London Bridge Renaissance Faire
One weekend in October
Tom Wilson
Crossroads Productions
P.O. Box 95, Riverside, CA 92502
(909) 943-5949
(800) 320-4REN
www.renaissanceinfo.com
renmail@renaissanceinfo.com

Tucson Celtic Festival & Scottish Highland Games
One weekend in November
Ora Beth Cesarini
PO Box 40665
Tucson, AZ 89717
(520) 883-1058
ernie.nelson@opt-sci.arizona.edu
tucson.com/TCFA

CALIFORNIA

Calaveras Celtic Festival
One weekend in March
Patrick Karnahan
PO Box 3995
Sonora, CA 95370
(209) 536-1792 or 532-8375
www.sonnet.com/celtic

Celebrate History
One weekend in April
Dana Lombardy
PO Box 70332
Pt. Richmond, CA 94807-0332
(800) 748-9901
(510) 595-0802
www.celebratehistory.com

Central Coast Renaissance Festival
One week in July
Larry Gunn
4921 Springwood Cir.
Cordelia, CA 94585
(800) 688-1477

Central Valley Renaissance Festival
One weekend in May
Larry Gunn
4921 Springwood Cir.
Cordelia, CA 94585
(800) 688-1477

Corona Renaissance Fantasy Faire
September-October
Tom Wilson
Crossroads Productions
P.O. Box 95
Riverside, CA 92502-0095
(909) 943-5949
(800) 320-4REN
www.renaissanceinfo.com
renmail@renaissanceinfo.com

Crossroads Renaissance Festival
One weekend in March
Tom Wilson
Crossroads Productions
P.O. Box 95
Riverside, CA 92502-0095
(909) 943-5949
(800) 320-4REN
www.renaissanceinfo.com,
renmail@renaissanceinfo.com

Day of St. Francis Renaissance Faire
One weekend in October
Mission San Luis Rey Parrish
4070 Mission Ave.
Oceanside, CA 92057
(760) 757-3250
www.SanLuisReyParrish.org

Dragonvale Medieval Carnival
One weekend in August
7657 Winnetka Ave., Ste. 502
Canoga Park, CA 91306
(661) 252-5662

European Renaissance Festival
April-May
Tom Wilson
Crossroads Productions
P.O. Box 95
Riverside, CA 92502-0095
(909) 943-5949
(800) 320-4REN
www.renaissanceinfo.com,
renmail@renaissanceinfo.com

Fair Oaks Renaissance Tudor Fayre
One weekend in June
Fair Oaks Rec and Parks
4150 Temescal St.
Fair Oaks, CA 95628
(916) 966-1036

Folsom Tournament & Renaissance Faire
One weekend in October
Christina Allen
Folsom Parks & Rec
50 Natoma St.
Folsom, CA 95630
(916) 355-7285

Fresno City College Renaissance Faire
One weekend in March
Michael Butler
P.O. Box 5621
Fresno, CA 93755
(559) 226-5341
MrVIII@aol.com

Hanford CA Renaissance of Kings Cultural Arts Faire
One weekend in October
Dolores Terrell
330 S. Bush Ave.
Fresno, CA 93727-4007
(559) 251-9257

Kearney Park Renaissance Faire
One weekend in November
(559) 227-5875

Long Beach Renaissance Arts Festival
One weekend in August
Ginny Swisher
2116 E. Force St.
Long Beach, CA 90814
(562) 438-9903

Mediterranean Renaissance Faire of Lake Tahoe
One weekend in June
Christine Karnofsky
ELFF Corp
PO Box 511
Tahoe Vista, CA 96148
(530) 546-5171
in CA: (877) 922-2223

Northwoods Renaissance Festival
One weekend in May
Bill Woodford
Win-River Casino
2100 Redding Rancheria Rd.
Redding, CA 96001
(800) 280-U-WIN

Ojai Renaissance Festival
One weekend in April
Richard Wixon
Gold Coast Productions
2509 Thousand Oaks Blvd.
Thousand Oaks, CA 91362
(805) 496-6036

Pittsburg's Scottish Renaissance Festival
One weekend in August
Highland Renaissance
Re-enactors Guild
c/o Richard Hills
4446 Palo Verde Dr.
Pittsburg, CA 94565
(925) 439-7343
HRRG@aol.com

Renaissance Harvest Festival
August–September
Ron Raushlaub
P.O. Box 349
Pescadero, CA 94060
(650) 879-1807

Renaissance Pleasure Faire, Spring
May-June
Renaissance Entertainment Corp
PO Box 9188
San Bernardino, CA 92427
(909) 880-6211
(for tix, call 800-52-FAIRE)
www.recfair.com

Santa Barbara Renaissance Faire
One weekend in September
Tom or Cheryl Cardoza
Living History Project
(805) 682-0310
www.sbrenfaire.com

Scandanavian Mid-Summer Festival
One weekend in June
Christian Nielsen, Pres.
Scandanavian Lodges
17 W. 14th Street
Eureka, CA 95501
(707) 445-8264

St. Paul Newman Center Renaissance Festival
One weekend in October
Judy Clifford
1572 E. Barstow
Fresno, CA 93710
(209) 436-3434

Tulare County Renaissance Festival
One weekend in April
Hudson Kent
Guild of St. Mortimer
1372 E. Finch Ave.
Tulare, CA 93274
(209) 688-0540
tulfair@prodigy.net

Valhalla Renaissance Festival
Two weekends in June
Steve Bailey
Tahoe Tallac Assoc.
3839 Oak Glen Dr.
Santa Rosa, CA 95404
(916) 542-4166

Prince Haulmlet's Prize Hens

by

David T. Orr

a wordy scop who hasn't finished it yet

One day, two poor, starving yard birds laid a breakfast for royalty. Quat could you well do, hence, except expect specks on a miserly mesne villein's plot, asked that fowl feudal task, to lay with udder loyalty ecru-flecked eggs over dew whene'er crude rooster crew?

"Rise early. Issue selects, or next nicht go the necks," Hodge the croft master mocked and scoffed. "Fancy she's granted any grain she can manage to ply herself chuck with? The plucky plump cluck's frock gets doffed faster once sly Sir Fox slicks his chops. Fancy the slop's chock full of pannage too sty sweet? Try dining on all fours, swine, or get klopped at another's whim!"

Now, when he heard how his fair-favored birds fared so meagerly, slender as slim Cinderella, whose splendor the Brothers Grimm rendered, our prince sent amain for this swain, who fled eagerly....

Willits Celtic Renaissance Faire
One weekend in May
Rich Venturi
1119 Madrone Cir.
Willits, CA 95490
(707) 459-3263
conor@zapcom.net

COLORADO

Colorado Renaissance Faire
June-August
Jim Paradise
409 S. Wilcox, Ste F
Castle Rock, CO 80104
(303) 688-6010

Grand River Renaissance & Fantasy Festival
One weekend in August
Carter & Lynn Reese
3212 Mesa Ave.
Clifton, CO 81520
(970) 523-7841

CONNECTICUT

Olde Worlde Renaissance Festival
One weekend in October
Dan Desilets
PO Box 36
Grosvenordale, CT 06246-0036
(860) 923-2421
producer@mythicaljourneys.com
www.mythicaljourneys.com/faire

FLORIDA

Bay Area Renaissance Festival
March-April
Mid-America Festivals
Lynn Knight
1244 Canterbury Rd. S. Ste 306
Shakopee, MN 55379-8944
(612) 445-7361

Hoggetowne Medieval Faire
One weekend in February
Linda Piper
P.O. Box 490, Station 30
Gainesville, FL 32602
(352) 334-5064
cultural@atlantic.com

The Italian Renaissance Festival at Vizcaya
One weekend in March
Bill Sims
7920 West Dr., Ste. 15
N. Bay Village, FL 33141
(305) 758-4595

Florida Keys Renaissance Faire
One weekend in January
Rose Stayduhar
P.O. Box 504306
Marathon, FL 33050
(305) 743-4386

Florida Renaissance Festival, South
February-March
Bobby Rodriguez Productions
801 NW 57th St.
Ft. Lauderdale, FL 33309-2826
(800) 3-RENFEST
renfest@aol.com
www.ren-fest.com

Florida Renaissance Festival, North
March-April
Bobby Rodriguez Productions
801 NW 57th St.
Ft. Lauderdale, FL 33309-2826
(800) 3-RENFEST
renfest@aol.com
www.ren-fest.com

Jacksonville Renaissance Faire
One weekend in January
Cynthia Riensche
St. John's Historical Event Corp.
1002 Barrs St.
Jacksonville, FL 32204
(904) 387-5238

Palm Beach Renaissance Festival
Two weekends in February
Mid-America Festivals
Bonnie Jacobson
1244 Canterbury Rd. S. Ste 306
Shakopee, MN 55379-8944
(800) 966-8215

Medieval Fair
One weekend in February
Mid-America Festivals
Bonnie Jacobson
1244 Canterbury Rd. S. Ste 306
Shakopee, MN 55379-8944
(800) 966-8215
(612) 445-7361

A Midwinter's Medieval Festival
One weekend in March
Tricia Noyes
Lake Como Nudist Resort
20500 Coot Rd.
Lutz, FL 33549
(813) 949-1810

GEORGIA

Georgia Renaissance Festival
Spring: April-June
Fall: October-November
Norma Pope
P.O. Box 986
Fairburn, GA 30213
(770) 964-8575

IDAHO

Chubbock Renaissance Faire
One weekend in September
Amy Lamb
Chubbock United Methodist Church
5147 Whitaker Rd.
Chubbock, ID 83202
(208) 237-5742

ILLINOIS

Jubilee College Olde English Faire
One weekend in June
Jim Trumminelli
11817 Jubilee College Rd.
Brimfield, IL 61517
(309) 243-9489

Southern Illinois Renaissance Festival
July-August
Aries Entertainment Group
PO Box 379
Hamel, IL 62046-0379
(217) 272-4424

Stronghold's Olde English Faire
One weekend in October
Stronghold Conference Center
Joy Butler-Mrkvicka
PO Box 199
Oregon, IL 61061
(815) 732-6111
www.essex1.com/people/strnghld

INDIANA

Indiana Renaissance Festival
One weekend in August
Greg Schmidt
Festivals Intl.
508 4th Ave. N.
Clear Lake, IA 50428
(515) 357-5177

Metea Renaissance Faire
One weekend in October
Allen County Park & Rec
7324 Yohne Rd.
Fort Wayne, IN 46809
(219) 449-3180
foxisland@mail.fwi.com

IOWA

Iowa Renaissance Festival and Harvest Faire
Two weekends in September
Greg Schmidt, Festivals Intl.
508 4th Ave. N.
Clear Lake, IA 50428
(515) 357-5177

Mount Vernon Olde World Faire
One weekend in May
Robert Meegan
307 3rd St SW
Mt. Vernon, IA 52314
(319) 895-8645

Renaissance Faire of the Midlands
One weekend in June
Sheri Wells-Chesley
PO Box 31134
Omaha, NE 68131-0134
(402) 345-5401

Salisbury Faire
One weekend in May
Salisbury House Foundation
4025 Tonawanda Dr.
Des Moines, IA 50312
(515) 274-1777

Wybreg Village Renaissance Faire
One weekend in June
Renaissance Foundation
304 15th St., Ste 314
Des Moines, IA 50309
(888) 243-4340

KANSAS

Kansas City Renaissance Festival
September-October
Melissa Vancrum
Mid-America Festivals
207 Westport Rd., Ste 206
Kansas City, MO 64111
(800) 373-0357
renfest@qni.com

Newman University Renaissance Faire
One weekend in April
Mike Casey
Newman University
3100 McCormick
Wichita, KS 67213
(316) 942-4291

KENTUCKY

Ravenhurst, a Medieval Fantasy
May-June
PO Box 54715
Lexington, KY 40505
(606) 276-0722

MAINE

Maine Renaissance Faire
July-August
Valerie Shute
Cloak & Dagger
12 Lewiston Rd.
New Gloucester, ME 04260
(207) 926-5693
Clkndggr@ime.net
www.mainefaire.com

MARYLAND

Hastings Battle and Medieval Faire
One weekend in October
Joe Carpenter
Markland Ltd.
PO Box 715
Greenbelt, MD 20768
(609) 779-1262
eogwls@hotmail.com

The Maryland Renaissance Festival
August-October
C.J. Crowe
Intl. Renaissance Festivals Ltd.
PO Box 315
Crownsville, MD 21032
(800) 296-7304
www.rennfest.com/mrf/Frame_Pages/index

MASSACHUSETTS

Hammond Castle Renaissance Faire
One weekend in July
Al Fairbrother
80 Hesperus Ave.
Gloucester, MA 01930
(508) 283 2080

Higgins Faire
One weekend in June
Higgins Armory Museum
Diane Laska-Nixon
100 Barber Ave.
Worcester, MA 01606
(508) 853-6015

King Richard's Faire
August-October
Bonnie Shapiro
King's Faire, Inc.
PO Box 419, Rt. 58
Carver, MA 02330
(508) 866-5391

MICHIGAN

Grand Traverse Renaissance Fair
One weekend in August
Melodie Linebaugh
Grand Traverse Pavillions
1000 Andrew Weiszner Dr.
Grand Traverse, MI 49604
(616) 932-3000

Michigan Renaissance Festival
August-September
Mid-America Festivals
Sherlynn Everly
1244 Canterbury Rd. S. Ste 306
Shakopee, MN 55379-8944
(800) 601-4848
members.aol.com/renfestmi/

Saline Celtic Festival
One weekend in July
Patrick Little
PO Box 590
Saline, MI 48176
(734) 429-0237

Silver Leaf Renaissance Festival
July- August
Box 2346
Portage, MI 49081
(616) 343-9090

MINNESOTA

Minnesota Renaissance Festival
August-September
Mid-America Festivals
Bonnie Jacobson
1244 Canterbury Rd. S. Ste 306
Shakopee, MN 55379-8944
(800) 966-8215

MISSOURI

Greater St. Louis Renaissance Faire
Two weekends in May
Doug Glenn
PO Box 148
Wentzville, MO 63385
(314) 916-1643

Hamlet of Slater Renaissance Festival of Mid-Missouri
One weekend in June
Melissa Alexander
Celtic Fire Productions
18999 Hwy CC
Houstonia, MO 65333
(660) 568-3536

MONTANA

University of Great Falls Renaissance Faire
One weekend in July
Lana Furdell
University of Great Falls
1301 20th St. S.
Great Falls, MT 59405
(406) 791-5255

NEVADA

Age of Chivalry Harvest Festival or Celtic Festival
One weekend in October
Fred McElhaney
Clark County Park & Rec.
2601 E. Sunset Rd.
Las Vegas, NV 89120
(702) 455-8289

NEW MEXICO

College of Santa Fe Renaissance Faire
One weekend in April
1600 St. Michael's Dr.
King Hall, Box 477
Santa Fe, NM 87505
(505) 473-6208

Dona Ana Arts Council Renaissance Craft Faire
One weekend in November
Judith Finch
Dona Ana Arts Council
224 N. Campo
Las Cruces, NM 88001
(505) 523-6403

Four Corners Renaissance Festival
One weekend in September
Diana Ohlsen
PO Box 3411
Farmington, NM 87499
sribb@cyberport.com

Silver City Renaissance Faire
September–October
Anna Stites
PO Box 1758
Silver City, NM 88062
(505) 388-9569
ravensong@gilanet.com
www.gilanet.com/renfaire

NEW JERSEY

New Jersey Renaissance Kingdom
May-June
Noreen Dunn
Dun-Ley Productions
P.O. Box 5683
Somerset, NJ 08875-5683
(732) 271-1119
dun-ley@njkingdom.com
www.NJKingdom.com

NEW YORK

Huntington Renaissance Faire
One weekend in May
Unitarian Universalists
109 Brown's Rd.
Huntington, NY 11743
(516) 427-9547

The Medieval Festival at Fort Tryon Park
One weekend in September
Eileen Merle
c/o WHIDC
57 Wadsworth Ave.
New York, NY 10033
(212) 795-1600
songbird.com@juno.com

New York Renaissance Faire
July-September
Joe Cargiulo
Renaissance Entertain. Corp.
600 Rte. 17A
Tuxedo, NY 10987
(914) 351-5171
www.renfair.com

Sterling Renaissance Festival
July-August
Virginia Young
15431 Farden Rd.
Sterling, NY 13156
(315) 947-5783
www.sterlingfestival.com

Woodstock Renaissance Faire
One weekend in May
Woodstock Ren. Faire
PO Box 901
Woodstock, NY 12498
(914) 679-7148

NORTH CAROLINA

Carolina Renaissance Festival
October-November
Jeffrey Siegel
PO Box 165
Davidson, NC 28036
(704) 896-5544

North Carolina Renaissance Festival
One weekend in March
Donna Varner
NC Renaissance Festival Inc.
5004 Whisper Ct.
Raleigh, NC 27616
(919) 755-8004

OHIO

Baycrafters Renaissance Fayre
One weekend in September
Sally Irwin Price
28795 Lake Rd.
Bay Village, OH 44140
(440) 871-6543

Great Lakes Medieval Faire
June-August
Susan Dunne
PO Box 251
Ashtabula, OH 44005
(888) MEDIEVAL

Medieval and Renaissance Faire at Ohio State Univ.
One weekend in May
CMRF c/o Karen Einstead
Dept. of English
421 Denney Hall
164 W. 17th Ave.
Columbus, OH 43210
Jason Abele: (614) 299-9840
abele.5@osu.edu
www.osu.edu/students/cmrf/

Ohio Renaissance Festival
August-October
Peter Carroll
P.O. Box 68
Harveysburg, OH 45032-0068
(513) 897-7000
ohio@renfestival.com
www.renfestival.com

Ravenwood Castle Spring Faire
One weekend in May
Sue Maxwell
Ravenwood Castle
65666 Bethel Rd.
New Plymouth, OH 45654
(740) 596-2606

Southeastern Ohio Renaissance Faire
One weekend in September
Nevertheless Productions
Joshua Brockwell
1008 Woodlawn Ave.
Cambridge, OH 43725
(740) 435-9338

Yuletide Revels in Merrie England
One weekend in December
Alumni Revels
Ohio Dominican College
1216 Sunbury Rd.
Columbus, OH 43219
(614) 251-4711

OKLAHOMA

The Castle at Muskogee Renaissance Faire
Two weeks in May
The Castle
3400 Fern Mountain Road
Muskogee, OK 74401
(918) 687-3625
the castle@thecastle.org
www.thecastle.org

Norman Medieval Faire
One weekend in April
Linda Linn
Univ. of Oklahoma
1700 Asp
Norman, OK 73072
(405) 288-2536
llinn@cce.occee.ou.edu
occe.ou.edu/medievalfair

Pendragon Faire
July-August
Oklahoma Renaissance Festival
Danny Reardon
413 W. Choctaw
Tahlequah, OK 74464
(816) 587-8597

OREGON

Dayes of Olde Medieval Festival
One weekend in August
Deanna
500 Lancaster Dr. SE
Salem, OR 97301
(503) 371-7375

Shrewsbury Renaissance Faire
One weekend in September
The Shrew
P.O. Box 604
Philomath, OR 97370
(541) 929-4897
shrew@peak.org

PENNSYLVANIA

Greater Pittsburgh Renaissance Festival
June-August
Lori Hughes
PO Box 1670
Greensburg, PA 15601
(724) 872-1670
info@pgh-renfest.com
www.pgh-renfest.com/festival

Pennsic War
(An SCA re-enactment)
One weekend in August
Pre reg: Fred Brezel
(724) 368-9309
www.whitebelt.com/pennsic

Pennsylvania Renaissance Faire
August–October
Barbara Lacek
Mount Hope Estate & Winery
P.O. Box 685
Cornwall, PA 17016
(717) 665-7021
www.parenaissancefaire.com

TENNESSEE

Drachenburg Renaissance Faire
October
Tina Plunk
544 Nashville Heights #311
Gallatin, TN 37066
(615) 841-3498
drachenburg@netzero.net

Tennessee Renaissance Festival
May
Mike Freeman
2124 New Castle Rd.
Arrington-Triune, TN 37014
(615) 395-9950

TEXAS

Columbus Fleet Renaissance Faire
One weekend in June
Columbus Fleet
1900 N. Chaparral
Corpus Christi, TX 78401
(361) 882-1232 Ext. 61

Excalibur Fantasy Faire
March-April
Jeanette Martin
1007 Main
Bastnop, TX 78602
(512) 303-3801
www.excalibur.com

Four Winds Renaissance Faire
March-April
Dustin Stephens
P.O. Box 1467
Whitehouse, TX 75791
(903) 842-2932
fourwinds@etgs.com

Hawkwood Medieval Fantasy Faire
August-September
James Echols
P.O. Box 3222
Grapevine, TX 76099
(800) 782-3629
members.aol.com/hawkwoodgg/hawkwood

San Antonio Spring Renaissance Faire
One weekend in May
Greg Schmidt
Festivals Intl.
508 4th Ave. N.
Clear Lake, IA 50428
(515) 357-5177

Scarborough Renaissance Faire
April-June
Southwest Festivals, Inc.
PO Box 538
Waxahachie, TX 75168
(972) 938-3247
TheRenFest@aol.com
www.scarboroughrenfest.com

Texas Renaissance Festival
October-November
Joseph P. Keyser
Rt. 2, Box 650
Plantersville, TX 77363
(800) 458-3435
www.texrenfest.com

West Texas Renaissance Faire
One week in October
2347 N. 6th St.
Abilene, TX 79603
(915) 672-3010
renfaire@camalott.com

Welcome to the World of Coins

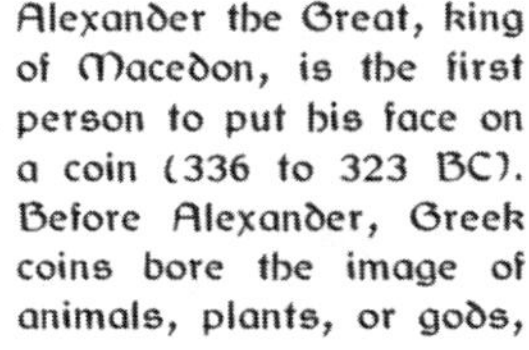

Alexander the Great, king of Macedon, is the first person to put his face on a coin (336 to 323 BC). Before Alexander, Greek coins bore the image of animals, plants, or gods, but no living people. Because Alexander had a large number of Celtic mercenaries in his army, the earliest Celtic coins follow Macedonian designs, like the example at right (300 to 100 BC).

The year of minting begins to appear on coinage in the late 15th Century. The first dated English coins appeear during the reign of Queen Elizabeth I. Every other silver denomination has the date stamped on it. (i.e., the 6p, 3p, 3/2p, and three-farthings are dated; the 12p, 4p, 2p, 1p, and halfpenny are not.) During the Renaissance, most coinage was hand-hammered, like the shilling at right. Machine-milled coins, like the sixpence above, were likewise a new innovation.

For FREE catalog of coins & antiquities, call or write to:

Money-Changers

P. O. Box 25595, Los Angeles, CA 90025

telephone: 323-342-9490

e-mail: moneychanger@earthlink.net

See us on the web at http://home.earthlink.net/~moneychanger

UTAH

Utah Midsummer Renaissance Faire
One weekend in July
Jack Tripp
P.O. Box 1443
Cedar City, UT 84721
(435) 586-1124
or Rick Bryant (435) 586-3711
(after 7 p.m.)

VERMONT

Medieval Days
One weekend in July
Dennis Seavey
RR1 Box 4513
Union, NH 03887
(603) 968-7197

King and the Mountain Tournament
One weekend in September
Dennis Seavey
RR3 Box 84E
Union, NH 03887
(603) 968-7197

VIRGINIA

Virginia Renaissance Faire
May-June
Ann Miller
Renaissance Entertain. Corp.
1175 Kings Hwy
Fredericksburg, VA 22405
(540) 371-3999
www.recfair.com

WASHINGTON

Camlann Medieval Faire
July-August
Roger Shell
Camlann Medieval Assoc.
10320 Kelly Rd. NE.
Carnation, WA 98104
(425) 788-1353

Gig Harbor Fantasy Faire
One weekend in August
Ronald Cleveland
12016 134th Ave KPN
Gig Harbor, WA 98329
(800) 359-5948
www.gigharborrenfaire.com

Kent Canterbury Faire
One weekend in August
Kent Parks and Rec.
220 4th Ave S.
Kent, WA 98032
(253) 859-3991

Northwest Renaissance Festival
July-August
Tienne Rogers
6493 Hwy 291
Nine Mile Falls, WA 99026
(509) 276-9169 or 487-2041
NorWstRF@aol.com

Ye Merrie Greenwood Renaissance Faire
One weekend in June
Marjorie Kunigisky
6015 W. 20th Ave.
Kennewick, WA 99338
(509) 783-7727
www.wizkeep.com

WISCONSIN

Audubon Wood Renaissance Faire
One weekend in September
Schlitz Audubon Center
1111 E. Brown Deer Rd.
Milwaukee, WI 53217
(414) 352-2880

Bristol Renaissance Faire
June-August
Shawn Johnson
Renaissance Entertain. Corp.
12550 120th Ave.
Kenosha, WI 53142-7337
(847) 395-7773
www.recfair.com

OUTSIDE THE U.S.

CANADA

International Jousting Tournament
One weekend in July
Quest for the Dragon's Blade
PO Box 1960
Port Elgin, Ontario N0H 2C0
(800) 361-0393
(519) 389-4441

Ontario Renaissance Festival
July-August
Intl. Renaissance Festivals, Ltd.
PO Box 486
Milton, Ontario CANADA
(800) 734-3779

Royal Medieval Faire
One weekend in September
City of Waterloo
100 Regina St. S.
Waterloo, ON N2J 4A8
CANADA
(519) 744-6058 or 883-0381
info@royalmedievalfaire.org
www.royalmedievalfaire.org

Stratford-on-the-Fraser Shakespeare Festival and Renaissance Faire
June-July
Lisa Chambers
34301 Norrish Ave.
Mission, BC V2V 6N9
CANADA
(604) 820-2717
jchambers@netcom.ca

Shakespeare Festivals

Alabama Shakespeare Festival
1 Festival Dr.
Montgomery, AL 36117
(334) 271-5353
www.asf.net

Atlantic Shakespeare Festival
July-August
PO Box 1975
St. Augustine, FL 32085
(904) 471-1965

Austin Shakespeare Festival
PO Box 683
Austin, TX 78767
(512) 454-BARD
members.aol.com/asf/

California Shakespeare Festival
June-October
The Bruns Amda Theatre
Gateway Boulevard
Orinda, CA
(510) 548-9666
www.calshakes.org

Colorado Shakespeare Festival
June-August
CSF Box Office
Campus Box 460
Boulder, CO 80309
(303) 492-0554

Fairbanks Shakespeare Theatre
PO Box 73447
Fairbanks, AK 99707
(907) 457-POET

Georgia Shakespeare Festival
June-December
4484 Peachtree Road N.E.
Atlanta, GA 03199
(404) 264-0020 or 504-3400
office@gashakespeare.org
www.gashakespeare.org

Idaho Shakespeare Festival
June-September
PO Box 9365
Boise, ID 83707
(208) 323-9700
www.idahoshakespeare.org

Illinois Shakespeare Festival
June-August
Box Office Campus Box 5700
Normal, ILL 61790-5700
(309) 438-2535

Lake Tahoe Shakespeare Festival
July-August
969 Tahoe Boulevard
Incline Village, NV 89451
(800) 747-4697
www.laketahoeshakespeare.com

New Jersey Shakespeare Festival
36 Madison Ave.
Madison, NJ 07940
(973) 408-3278
www.njshakespeare.org

Oregon Shakespeare Festival
Feb.-Oct.
PO Box 158
Ashland, OR 97520
(541) 482-4221
www.orshakes.org

Shakespeare Santa Cruz
July-August
Terri Fette
UCSC Performing Arts Center
1156 High St
Santa Cruz, CA 95064
(831) 459-2159
shakespearesantacruz.org

Washington Shakespeare Festival
May-August
Leslie VanLeishout
PO Box 1501
Olympia, WA 98507
(360) 943-9492

OUTSIDE THE U.S.

CANADA

Victoria Shakespeare Festival
July-August
P.O. Box 8796
Victoria BC V8W 353
(250) 360-0234
tinconnu@islandnet.com
www.island.com/~tinconnu

Bard on the Beach
June-Sept.
1101 W. Broadway
Vancouver, BC V6H 1G2
(604) 739-0559
www.faximum.com/bard/

Faire Performers

Broon
Brian Howard
1110 Westview Terr
Laurel, MD 20707
(301) 332-2802
brun020102@aol.com
members.aol.com/bruno20102/

Clan Dummunhull Gypsy Magic and Variety Show
Happy Toad Entertainment
(714) 903-1566
cyran01@aol.com or CDGypsy@xoommail.com
members.xoom.com/CDGypsy

Crossed Swords
Nicole Harsch and Mike Sakuta
sword@swordmark.com
www.deathstar.org/~sword/

Dagger Dan
www.daggerdan.com

Jeffrey the Traveling Juggler
Jeffrey Daymont
PO Box 4931
Long Beach, CA 90804
(562) 987-4237
yeajeffrey@aol.com

Hack and Slash
Nigel Hack and Slash Montant
5765F Nurke Centre Pkwy, Ste. 125
Burke, VA 22015
www.hackandslash.com
mail@hackandslash.com

RatCatcher
Emerys Fleet
emerysfleet@earthlink.net
home.earthlink.net/emerysfleet/

The Royal Chessmen
(305) 661-0425
www.RoyalChessmen.com

The Sturdy Beggars Mud Show
Billy Billy von Billy
Hack Ptui
Rott Wyler
Half-Wit Henry
(630) 415-3354
billy@mudshow.com
www.mudshow.com

The Tortuga Twins
D'Angelo Tortuga (Jeff Hall)
Scaramouche Tortuga (Ronn Bauman)
Raphael Tortuga (Riki Robinson)
(813) 867-6507
jeff@tortugatwins.com
www.tortugatwins.com

Zoltan
Andy Blau
(416) 783-8796
blaupunk@justadequate.com
www.justadequate.com

The Zucchini Brothers
Ripe and Green
(770) 969-2300
www.velocity.net/~goforit/zuke

Resources

European Costume: 4000 Years of Fashion
by Doreen Yarwood
Bonanza Books, 1975

A World Lit Only by Fire
by William Manchester
Back Bay Books, 1993

Heraldry: An Introduction to a Noble Tradition
by Michael Pastoureau
Discoveries / Harry Abrams, 1997

The Public and Private Worlds of Elizabeth I
by Susan Watkins
Thames & Hudson, 1998

The Mammoth Book of British Kings and Queens
by Mike Ashley
Carroll & Graf, 1998

The Writer's Guide to Everyday Life in Renaissance England
by Kathy Lynn Emerson
Writer's Digest Books, 1996

On This Day in History
by Leonard and Thelma Spinrad
Prentice Hall Books, 1999

Greenwich 2000 Network
greenwich2000.com

The Tudor Times
www.tudor.simplenet.com

Chapel Hill Celtic Society
ils.unc.edu/christie/days

Feudal Terms of England
wiretap.spies.com/00/Library/Article/Socio/feudal.dic

Photographic Information

Page 2: Queen Eleanor, Michigan Renaissance Festival; **Page 4:** Simplicity Pattern Co., Pattern #8192; **Page 6:** Queen Elizabeth I, Kansas City Renaissance Festival; **Page 8:** Robert Dudley (aka Jay Boulton), The Guild of St. Olaf's; **Page 10:** Queen Anne of Cleves, Texas Renaissance Festival, **Page 12:** Lady Elizabeth Throckmorton (aka Anastasia Rutherford) and Master Francis Manners (aka Dan Rutherford); **Page 14:** Queen Elizabeth I, S. California Pleasure Faire; **Page 16:** The Comedic Duo Hack and Slash; **Page 18:** Museum Replicas item #MR18033; **Page 20:** Simplicity Pattern Co., Pattern # 8249; **Page 22:** Lady and the Earl of Pembroke (aka Anna and George Morris), The Guild of St. Olaf's; **Page 24:** Queen Elizabeth I, Sterling Renaissance Festival, NY, Queen Katherine, King Richard's Faire, MA, Queen Eleanor, Arizona Renaissance Festival; **Page 26:** Lord Burghley (aka Howard Lorton), The Guild of St. Olaf's; **Page 28:** Simplicity Pattern Co., Pattern #8192; **Page 30:** Lady Radcliffe, Countess of Sussex and Sir Thomas Radcliffe, Earl of Sussex, Guild of St. George, Virginia Renaissance Faire; **Page 32:** King Henry VIII, Texas Renaissance Festival; **Page 34:** Queen Elizabeth I, Virgina Renaissance Faire; **Page 36:** Simplicity Pattern Co., Pattern #8192; **Page 38:** Simplicity Pattern Co., Pattern #7756; **Page 40:** Miguel (aka Doug Kondziolka) of Don Juan and Miguel, Texas Renaissance Festival; **Page 42:** Museum Replicas item #MR19693; **Page 44:** Sir Lancelot (aka Tom Davies) and Sir Bors (aka Clint Gidwell) of Event Productions, LCC; **Page 46:** King Henry VIII and the Queen of France, The Maryland Renaissance Festival; **Page 48:** DZM, St. Helen's Guild, N. California Pleasure Faire; **Page 50:** Museum Replicas item #MR18002; **Page 52:** Merlin (aka Don Evans) of Event Productions, LCC; **Page 54:** The Great Antoine, Texas Renaissance Festival; **Page 56:** Queen Elizabeth I, Ohio Renaissance Festival; **Page 58:** Museum Replicas item #MR19915; **Page 60:** Sir Gawain (aka Pete Cuppage) and Sir Gareth (aka Sean Rao) of Event Productions, LCC; **Page 62:** Barbarian Toruk, Texas Renaissance Festival; **Page 64:** Museum Replicas item #MR18034; **Page 66:** Ambassador Neville Ravenswood, Guild of St. George, Virginia Renaissance Faire; **Page 68:** Princess Isolde (aka Alana Fulcher and Sir Triston (aka Cliff Lawson) of Event Productions, LCC; **Page 70:** Texas Renaissance Festival; **Page 72:** King Johan Wasa III (aka Ole Olausson) and Lady Susanna Shakespeare (aka Kerri Dillon), The Guild of St. Olaf's; **Page 74:** Winifreid Rich, Lady North, Baroness North of Kirtling, Guild of St. George, Virginia Renaissance Faire; **Page 76:** Museum Replicas item #MR19145; **Page 78:** Simplicity Pattern Co., Pattern #8735, trimmings by Simplicity Trims Collection; **Page 80:** Mary Stuart, Queen of Scots (aka Susan Carol Abernethy) and James Hepburn, Earl of Bothwell (aka Robert Persons); **Page 82:** Lady Nimue (aka Toni Baker) of Event Productions, LCC; **Page 84:** Museum Replicas item #MR19741; **Page 86:** Simplicity Pattern Co., Pattern #18725; **Page 88:** Sir Henry Sydney, Knight of the Garter, Guild of St. George, Virginia Renaissance Faire; **Page 90:** Museum Replicas item #MR19635; **Page 92:** Simplicity Pattern Co., Pattern #8881; **Page 94:** King Henry the Only at The Arizona Renaissance Festival, The Minnesota Renaissance Festival, and The Carolina Renaissance Festival; **Page 96:** Museum Replicas item #MR18012; **Page 98:** Queen Katherine the Only, Minnesota Renaissance Festival; **Page 100:** Museum Replicas item #MR19615; **Page 102:** Simplicity Pattern Co., Pattern #8725, trimmings by Conso Princess Collection and Elizabethan Range; **Page 104:** Museum Replicas item #MR19887; **Page 106:** Simplicity Pattern Co., Pattern #8192 and 8249

Acknowledgements

Michelle Young of Adah Rose Advertising, for
Museum Replicas
Box 840
Conyers, GA 30012
(800) 883-8838

Alison
Simplicity Pattern Co. Inc.
2 Park Ave.
New York, NY 10016

Thomas M. Krekow
The Image Group
905 Broadway
Kansas City, MO 64105
(816) 421-4990

Linda Clark and the Guildmembers of St. George
The Virginia Renaissance Festival

Photographer Allen DeRico (562) 693-5533
and the Guildmembers of St. Olaf's

Shown Nichols
The Texas Renaissance Festival

All Renaissance Festivals that generously provided us with photos of their performers

...and last but not least, Sir Miles of Rohan, Michael J. Warhola, and Alma Jill Dizon

**Have we missed an important historical date of note?
If so, please contact us at:**

RENAISSANCE MAGAZINE
80 Hathaway Drive
Stratford, CT 06615-7304